CHARMED

FAIRY TALE
REFORM SCHOOL

CHARMED

JEN CALONITA

SCHOLASTIC INC.

ISBN 978-1-338-04833-9

Copyright © 2016 by Jen Calonita.
Cover and internal design copyright © 2016 by Sourcebooks, Inc.
Cover image by Mike Heath/Shannon Associates. All rights reserved.
Published by Scholastic Inc., 557 Broadway, New York, NY 10012, by arrangement with Sourcebooks Jabberwocky, an imprint of Sourcebooks, Inc. SCHOLASTIC and associated logos are trademarks and/or registered trademarks of Scholastic Inc.

12 11 10 9 8 7 6 5 4 3   17 18 19 20 21

Printed in the U.S.A.   40

First Scholastic printing, April 2016

For Elpida Argenziano, the strongest, bravest princess I know.

Sometimes it's good to be bad.

WANTED

Alva the Wicked Fairy

Reward for the capture of Alva, better known as Sleeping Beauty's dreamcaster

Alva was last seen fleeing Fairy Tale Reform School. The fairy's dark magic makes her dangerous in any form. (She can transform herself into a fire-breathing dragon *and* an old hag.) Alva is rumored to be recruiting an army to help her take over the kingdom of Enchantasia. *You* can make sure this does not happen! If you hear of her whereabouts, alert the Dwarf Police Squad immediately.

REWARD: 10,000 gold pieces

*This message approved by the Royal Court

Happily Ever After Scrolls

Brought to you by FairyWeb—magically appearing on scrolls throughout Enchantasia for the past ten years!

Where Is the Thorn in Sleeping Beauty's Side Hiding?

by Coco Collette

It's hard to believe that it's been two months since Princess Rose, our favorite sleeping beauty, found out that her evil fairy, Alva, is not only alive but has been plotting to take over Enchantasia. Alva reappeared at the fifth anniversary ball for Fairy Tale Reform School, the school for wicked or criminally mischievous fairy-tale students. While Alva was unsuccessful in her takeover (whew!), she was able to turn Professor Harlow villainous once more. (Guess we can start calling her the Evil Queen again.) Harlow was taken into custody and is being held in the dungeons at FTRS, but Alva escaped.

"I thought I had seen the last of that fairy, and now she's back to torture not only me, but also my beloved kingdom," says Princess Rose. "I won't stop 'til Alva is brought to justice and my citizens are safe once more. We're lucky Gillian Cobbler was there to help save us."

Gillian, an FTRS student and the daughter of village shoemaker Hal Cobbler, rescued a ballroom full of students, royals, and citizens from Alva. Praise for Gillian has come from villagers and princesses alike. Neil at Combing the Sea says Team Gilly shirts are flying off his shelves. "A comb plucked from my shop got Gilly thrown into FTRS in the first place," says Neil proudly.

The royals were so pleased that they gave Gilly's father his job back making glass slippers for the royal families. Ever since, orders have flooded into Hal's shop from as far away as Parrington and Captiva. "I just ordered a pair of Hal's brand-new glass-slipper high tops," says Rapunzel, who plans on wearing them in an ad for her new hair-care products. "They're comfortable yet stylish. What more could a princess ask for?"

How about safety? Sources say Princess Rose has been unsettled by Alva's reemergence and feels the royal court has not been doing enough to find the evil fairy. The sleepy princess is said to have fled the castle in a huff and is spending time at FTRS as a mentor to the famed Royal Ladies-in-Waiting Club.

Keeping checking your Happily Ever After Scrolls *for more coverage on Alva!*

CHAPTER 1

Charm School

Miri's voice crackles through the magic mirrors in Fairy Tale Reform School. "Let the first annual Wand What You Want hour begin!"

Wands begin popping up in kids' hands as we walk through the halls, and we all cheer. *Pop!* My wand arrives in my hand—long, dark gray, and nicked like it's seen a few battles. Hmm...what to try first... I'm just about to test the wand out when I feel the hair on the back of my neck stand up. Instinct tells me to dive out of the way. When I look up, I see a classmate spelling the troll next to her. The girl turns into an ice sculpture. Geez, that was close. I better stay alert.

Pop! Pop! Pop! Kids begin casting all around me. The crowded hallway is suddenly full of talking woodland creatures, toads, fireworks, and a pretty impressive cloud raining licorice. Kids are cheering and fighting, and the sound of all those wands working is enough to give me a headache. I hurry away from the spell zapping, looking for somewhere to practice alone.

Slurp!

The chaotic hallway disappears behind me, and a new empty hall arrives in its place. I happen to know this hall leads to the school courtyard so I hurry down it and head outside. Ahhh…this is more like it. The warm sun is shining bright high above the castle walls, making me wistful for adventure. I can never sit still for long.

"Pardon the interruption! We hope you are enjoying your wand experience, but remember, all wands disappear at the hour mark so choose your magic wisely," Miri says. I'm relieved to find no mirror in the courtyard, which means she can't see what I'm up to. That magic mirror is forever tattling on students for bad behavior. "As a reminder, flying is not advised."

"Not advised, but she didn't say it was against the rules," I say to myself. I flick the wand over my stuffy, uncomfortable pale-blue uniform and turn it into a comfy peasant shirt and pants. I swap out my ugly school shoes for my beloved lace-up boots. Now that I'm comfortable, I get to the task at hand. I'm sure an actual spell would work better, but since I don't know one, I just imagine myself flying and—*bam!* I'm slowly floating up, up, up in the air. *Score!*

A Pegasus flies by me pulling a coach with four students in it. "*Hi, Gilly!*" they shout and wave.

When you save your school from a wicked fairy, people tend to remember your name. Even if you don't remember theirs.

"Hi!" I say, lying back like I'm floating on a cloud. *Wow, this is relaxing.* I stretch my arms wide and—*oops!*

My wand falls from my grasp. *Uh-oh.* I begin to plummet, spinning faster and faster with no sign of stopping. Before I can even think of a way to break my fall, *whoosh!* I feel my body hit a blanket and bounce up, then land again on a magic carpet.

"Ten minutes into Wand What You Want, and you're already having a near-death experience?" my friend Jax asks. His curly blond hair looks white in the bright sunlight. He casually waves his own wand in my direction with a glint in his violet eyes. "You're getting sloppy."

"I'm not getting sloppy!" I'm seriously offended by that statement. "How'd you even know where to find me?"

"I thought to myself, 'What would Gilly do with wand access for an hour?' and I knew right away you'd try to sneak home for a bit," Jax says. "Let's give it a go, shall we?"

My usual partner in crime steers our magic carpet over the castle walls and across the vast school grounds. Below I can see students fanned out on castle rooftops, in the garden mazes, and near the lake, all casting away with various results. Jax flies the carpet faster, the wind whipping our hair and making it hard to see. I push the hair away from my eyes and strain to see home.

There beyond the silver turrets of Royal Manor, where the princesses who rule our kingdom live, is my small village of Enchantasia. Somewhere down there, my family is working, playing, and hopefully missing me as much as I miss them. The carpet is nearing the Hollow Woods—which separates us and the village—and I lean forward. It's going to happen. We're going to leave school and see them! Closer we fly to the treetops...closer to the forest filled with ogres... closer to leaving school grounds when—*CRACKLE!*

Our magic carpet is suddenly stunned by an invisible wall that keeps us from escaping the school grounds. A magical scroll drops from the sky into our laps. "Leaving school grounds is forbidden!" it says in sparkling script that glows red like a warning. "Please return to the castle at once!" It's signed "Headmistress Flora."

"Smooth, Flora," Jax says. "Putting a barricade in the sky during wand training was clever."

"Leaving was a long shot, but maybe I could wave my wand and at least see what my family is up to," I say and gasp. "My wand! I need to go get it."

"Lose something, Gilly?" Our friend Maxine pilots a small flying swan boat I recognize from the Mother Goose carnival that was at school this past weekend. How does Maxine have one of those boats? Hmm… Bigger question: What's she doing in midair? Ogres don't usually like to be off the ground.

Maxine's right eye spins in its socket as she makes her way toward us with a crooked smile. Her thick neck is covered in layers of necklaces and the jewels she used to like to steal. (That's how she got thrown in FTRS. My offense was pickpocketing and shoplifting.) Maxine tosses the wand toward me but it's snatched away.

"Come and get it!" Jax's roommate, Ollie, shouts. He's flying on the back of a black baby dragon, which does not seem smart. Ollie dives back toward the courtyard and Jax, Maxine, and I follow, landing seconds later in the courtyard I left only minutes before. I jump off the carpet and grab my wand from Ollie before his baby dragon can eat it. But I don't need to worry because—*poof!*—the dragon disappears.

"A baby dragon on school grounds?" My roommate, Kayla, waves her wand in the air dangerously, and I worry about what she could zap next. Her wings pop out of her back and she flutters to Ollie's side. As a fairy, Kayla can shrink to the size of a teacup, but at the moment, she towers over Ollie, white-blond hair whipping in the wind. "That thing could burn down the whole school."

"We've already had that almost happen," Jax jokes. "Let's not do it again."

"Fine," Ollie says dejectedly. "I really wanted a pet." His eyes light up. "Snack break!" He waves his wand at the ground and conjures up an apple pie as big as the magic carpet I was just on. *Poof!* He also creates a supersize ice cream sundae and a plate of cookies as big as Maxine. He waves the wand again and a picnic basket, blanket, and plates appear on the grass beside it. "Let's eat!"

"We could use some ambiance," says Kayla who quickly transforms a dead rosebush into a beautiful plant with eye-popping roses in shades of fuchsia, electric blue, and lime green. Kayla flutters over to the blanket to help Ollie dish out dessert. He's using his wand as a cake knife and slicing pieces as big as my arm.

"Don't forget the music," says Maxine. She waves her wand in the air, and a flock of birds appears on a tree above us. They begin to chirp and hum in harmony. "*Yes!* It worked!" Maxine trudges over to the blanket happily, her ogre feet leaving deep footprints in the grass.

"Flora must have lost her mind to let a bunch of reform-school kids use wands for an hour," Jax says, flashing me a smile so blinding that I wish I had shades.

Poof! I use my wand to conjure up a pair. *Sweet!* I wish we could use wands every day instead of just in How a Wand Works 101. Madame Camille, our uptight fairy teacher, never lets us sign them out for homework, and every time someone screws up by zapping off their pinkie or growing their nose to three times its size, she says, "This is why Enchantasia doesn't allow wands 'til you're twenty-one!"

If I'd had a wand when I lived in the village, I wouldn't

have had to steal food to help feed my brothers and sisters in our overcrowded boot. I could have just conjured up the finest treats Gnome-olia Bakery had to offer with a flick of my wrist. Then I wouldn't have been sentenced to Fairy Tale Reform School. From the outside, this place looks like your average school. But inside we have hallways that move every time you use them, a talking magic mirror who tattles on you if you step out of line, a class taught by a mer-teacher inside a giant fish tank, and professors who all are former villains. How do you like them poison apples?

FTRS is nothing like that snooze-fest shoemaker trade school I used to attend and will have to go back to when I prove I have transformed my villainous ways into upstanding ones. Some days—when villains aren't trying to kill me—I'm bummed about being sprung from this joint. Especially when I think about leaving this crew.

"Look, I get Flora disappearing to help Professor Wolfington suppress his wolf side again, but where has she been since he came back?" Jax continues. "We never see her around school, and now she's letting us take wands out for a spin? Something's up."

"I'm with Jax," Maxine says, apple oozing down her chin

as she chews. "My mini magical scroll has been showing me weird messages like 'She'll reappear when you're all distracted' instead of articles from *Happily Ever After Scrolls*."

Ollie gives me a look. Maxine swears her mini magical scroll is sending her messages, but mini magical scrolls only report the daily Enchantasia news. She seems to think her scroll is magical. Okay, *more* magical.

"Yesterday it said, 'Prepare. She is coming soon.'" Maxine cuts another slice of pie for herself that is as big as her head. "Who is coming? Flora? I quickly hid my scroll since I was supposed to be doing homework."

"I think Flora is just trying to give us some freedom," I say. "If they don't give us freedom every now and then, how are they going to see whether we're reforming?"

"Yeah, Maxine. Can't you just be happy we have an afternoon off from Villain to Hero: How to Make the Switch?" Kayla asks.

Maxine frowns. "I actually kind of miss Dragon Slaying 101, but sometimes learning about a dragon's weak spots is enough to make me want to breathe fire."

I sit up. "That gives me an idea." I begin to aim my wand but Jax stops me.

"I'm serious, guys," Jax says quietly. "Alva's on the loose, someone is spilling royal secrets, and Flora keeps disappearing. Don't you want to know what's going on?"

Jax is an undercover royal at a reform school. Of course he wants to sort things out and go back to being all royally. (He is secretly Rapunzel's brother, not that she knows that. She thinks he's off at boarding school, and Jax's dad had the royal court's memories bewitched so no one recognizes him.) And yes, I want to go home to my family, but in the past two months I've saved royals, kept our school from burning down, and had T-shirts made with my name on them. I need a short recess to relax.

"Can't we take an hour off from being good guys and enjoy doing something a bit wicked?" I conjure up Jax's favorite pie—figgy pudding—and his eyes go wide. "Let's eat before we plot!"

My friends and I begin slicing up the desserts in front of us when *poof!* They disappear right in front of our eyes.

"*Hey!*" Ollie's fork hangs in the air over a now-empty plate. "Who did that?"

I look around the courtyard. Through the stained glass windows inside the school, I can see flashes of light every time a wand is used. Some hallways are filled with water where mermaids swim with ease and students have transformed into sharks and octopuses. Other windows show students dressed like princesses and pirates, while another set of windows shows mischief that could get those kids detention for a week with Madame Cleo. But I couldn't see a single person pointing a wand our way.

Then I hear a sinister laugh. I exhale sharply and look closer at my surroundings. I point my wand directly at the black gargoyle statue near the courtyard door that I don't remember seeing earlier. The statue starts to spark and then it transforms into a girl with long, dark hair in a black dress covered with stars and moons.

"Ouch! That hurt!" Jocelyn rubs her butt, which has a burn mark on one of the half-moons. "You singed my dress!"

"You stole our dessert." I wave my wand, wondering what I could do to Jocelyn next. Turn her into a toad? Make her wear a pink princess dress since she's allergic to any color but black? Lock her in a tower to keep her from casting any more spells?

"Sorry for the interruption, students," Miri's voice is back over the magical loudspeaker system. "Headmistress Flora would like me to remind you that illegal use of magic—such as escape attempts, turning your roommate into a toad, or using wand work for monetary gain—is not allowed. Today's Wand What You Want experiment is to see how you handle having a bit of wand freedom. Remember that. Thank you!"

Fiddlesticks.

"Did you want to join us?" Maxine asks awkwardly. She may be slightly afraid of the Evil Queen's little sister, but I'm not. Professor Harlow is now tucked away in the FTRS dungeons. Why Headmistress Flora allowed Jocelyn to stay in school is beyond me.

"She's not welcome here," I say calmly. "Give our food back."

Jocelyn shrugs. "Make me."

I use my wand to make the food reappear.

Jocelyn zaps it and makes it disappear.

I bring the food back.

Jocelyn makes it vanish.

Appear, disappear, appear, disappear.

Finally I snap. With my wand high above my head, I lift Ollie's giant apple pie and let the whole thing drop on Jocelyn's head. She screams. "Score!" I shout.

"Gilly, don't start with her," Kayla says, growing nervous. She's still a bit jittery around villains. I can't say I blame her. She was blackmailed by Alva for years, forced to help the evil fairy in exchange for information on the whereabouts of her missing family. (Who are now trees. It's complicated.)

"I'm fine!" I say, but while I'm laughing, Jocelyn is conjuring. *Smack!* A piece of pudding pie flies into my face.

"How does the pudding taste, Cobbler?" Jocelyn taunts. "I bet you guys could never afford pudding in your boot."

"We can now, while you're an orphan with an evil sister in lockup." I shoot a cherry pie at her face. It explodes and covers her with cherries. *Hee.* I look to Kayla for approval, but that "orphan" comment leaves her cold. Okay, maybe that was a bit harsh. I'm so busy staring at Kayla that I don't feel the crackle 'til it's too late.

"My hair!" I screech as my head begins to glow for a second, then stops. I feel my hair. It's all still there. I exhale. "Ha! Your spell didn't work!" I sing out.

"Um, Gilly?" Ollie asks. "Did you always have a purple streak in your hair?"

I pull the front of my hair forward and gasp. A deep

purple stripe is now running through my long, brown hair. Jocelyn bursts out laughing.

"Change it back!"

Jocelyn shrugs. "Can't. I didn't spell you. I cursed you. It can't be undone."

"Why you…" *Zap!* I send a vat of chocolate ice cream raining down on her head.

"Enough!" Ollie says as a wall of dead fish smacks him in the face, leaving a slimy trail on his light-brown skin.

"You can't do that." Jax sounds funny holding his nose. He quickly conjures up a massive bowl of cooked spinach, which hits Jocelyn with a loud *splat*.

Soon food is flying through the air like hail. Broccoli is raining from the rooftop. Mashed potatoes create walls we can use as barricades. Radishes hit Kayla in the head and give her welts. We're so busy conjuring up food that we don't hear the sound at first.

KABOOM!

The noise and the low rumble that follows are enough to make us all jump.

Kayla wipes stew from her hair. "What was that?" She sounds worked up.

Jocelyn spits out cherry pits that have appeared in her mouth. "Don't get your wings twisted. I'm sure Professor Biggins just misfired a potion he was working on."

"If there was a reason to panic, the alarms would have gone off." I listen carefully.

KABOOM!

This time the sound is so loud that we grab each other to keep from falling.

WOO-OOH! WOO-OOH!

The school security system is going off. Seconds later, our wands disappear along with the picnic, Maxine's swan boat, magic carpet, and my comfy clothes. My dreaded uniform is back, but that's not my biggest concern. I know what we're all thinking: the last time the alarm tripped was when we had a break-in from Alva.

"I'm going," I say and head toward the courtyard door.

"So am I." Jocelyn tries to beat me to the doorway. We each try to push the other out of the way.

I push her back. "You just want the distraction to help your sister escape the dungeons. I'm not going to let you help her!"

"Try to stop me!" Jocelyn pushes me so hard that I fall. I quickly jump up and follow her into the hallway. It's chaos.

Students are running in every direction, but I follow Jocelyn's food-splattered dress. I can hear my friends calling me, but I don't stop.

"Students, this is Headmistress Flora speaking." I hear Cinderella's formerly wicked stepmother's voice ring out from the castle's mirrors. "Please proceed to your dorm rooms. We have the situation under control. There is no cause for alarm."

A hallway switches in front of me, but I dive through it and land right on top of Jocelyn. We're somehow outside again—the new hallway leads us to the school lake.

KABOOM!

"Ouch!" Jocelyn yells as my friends fly out of yet another hallway, dropping onto the same grassy patch near the water.

"Holy shipwreck!" Ollie says, pointing to something in the distance on the water. I hear a commotion and shouting. "Duck!"

We drop to the ground just in time to see a cannonball whiz past our heads.

"Um, guys?" Kayla's frown deepens. "What's a pirate ship doing in the *lake* at Fairy Tale Reform School?"

CHAPTER 2

Ye Be a New Teacher in Town

Jocelyn and I stop fighting long enough to take in the giant pirate ship that has appeared in our school lake. The worn, wooden ship is so large it takes up almost the entire body of water. A tattered black-and-white flag bearing a skull and crossbones is flying high along another flag with a crest full of swords. Dozens of pirates race around the ship deck pulling ropes and they're calling out orders that I can't understand.

The mer-folk at school seem just as bewildered as we are because their heads start popping up around the lake to see what is going on. They point to the creepy serpent-headed gold figure carved into the prow of the ship, and then many disappear again below the dark waters.

"Land ho!" A pirate with a telescope yells from the ship's crow's nest. "We've arrived at Fairy Tale Reform School, captain!" A giant anchor is quickly tossed from the side of the ship and almost clocks a mer-boy in the head. Then I see a group of pirates lowering a gangplank.

"I can't believe it." Ollie is freaking out below me. (He's kind of short, swarthy, and a tad stocky...much like the pirates coming off the ship.) "I really can't believe it! Do you know whose ship that is?" he asks, starting to wind up like one of my little brother's toys. "I've always wanted to see it. It's legendary. *Legendary.* The pirate ship I was on is nowhere near as big as this one!"

Ollie's in FTRS because he used magic tricks for monetary gain. (I have to say, his sleight-of-hand maneuvers are amazing.) He says he learned everything he knows from his time as a stowaway on a pirate ship, but a lot of classmates say his pirate claims are tall tales. He's never been able to offer any actual proof that he was a short-term pirate.

"You see that large patched hole in the side of the ship?" Ollie asks. "They got hit racing away from the Royal Navy after pillaging the gold taxes the navy had collected from a port. The Brits never caught up with them, and legend has it the pirates used the gold to buy their own island." Ollie sighs. "That pirate knows how to make things happen."

"Who are you blabbering about?" Jocelyn snaps.

Ollie looks stunned. He points at the lake. "You mean you really don't recognize the ship?"

The gangplank drops with a thud right in front of us. Pirates begin disembarking, swinging their swords menacingly in the air.

"Um, guys? Should we get out of here?" Maxine asks as I hear a *slurp* sound from behind us.

"Ah, he's finally arrived and, of course, with much fanfare," I hear a familiar voice say in her classic clipped tone. It's a voice she uses right before shipping students off to detention. "I thought I told him no cannon fire on school grounds!"

Our teachers have arrived. Headmistress Flora (a.k.a. the former wicked stepmother of Cinderella who runs our school) leads the way, accompanied by Professor Wolfington (a.k.a. the Big Bad Wolf). Madame Cleo (a beautiful mermaid who is the sea siren that gave the Little Mermaid all that trouble) swims up to a nearby rock at the water's edge.

Professor Wolfington sees me and gives a wolfish grin. "I see our new colleague has a welcome wagon. Hello, students."

"Professor Wolfington!" Maxine says with glee. "You're back!"

He scratches his scruffy beard, which is tame compared to his long mane of wild hair and the dark fur on his hands. "You didn't think I'd stay away forever, did you?"

"We weren't sure you'd be able to come back after getting all…" Maxine bears her ogre teeth and gnashes the air while making her hands like claws. "You know."

Maxine means Professor Wolfington went full-blown Big Bad Wolf werewolf-style at the fifth anniversary ball to help save us from Alva. The rumor around school was that once our history teacher transformed to his dark side again, he could never return.

"Miss Maxine, everyone has setbacks now and then, but with discipline and reflection, we can continue on a path of virtue." Professor Wolfington sounds like he's reciting from our psychology textbook *Wickedly Good in 30 Days or Less*.

"Maxine, it is not appropriate to question your teachers," Headmistress Flora reprimands. Flora's tiny eyes are dark, much like the black in her black-and-white hair, which is swept up in a bun. "Professor Wolfington's training has taught him how to bounce back from any, shall we say, wolf-ish situation. Not that he needs to explain himself."

"It's fine, Flora," Professor Wolfington says pleasantly. "I took some time off for reflection, and now I'm back to meet my interesting new colleague."

"What be ye all caterwauling about?" asks the heavyset pirate approaching us.

He's dressed in a dingy jacket and ripped pants; a spar-kling silver sword hangs from the leather holster on his hip. His head is covered by a beat-up pirate hat with a little skull and crossbones stamped on the front. His long, bushy hair is almost jet-black, and his full beard has several beaded braids that swing as he talks. "Wolfie, good to see you." The two shake hands, and I notice the pirate's fingernails are almost black. He turns to Headmistress Flora, who could not be dressed more differently than him in a button-down dress with a full petticoat.

"Flora, you sly lassie, me thinks ye didn't give me the real tale on this school of yers," bellows the pirate. "This castle be way bigger than ye described. Ye must have stole a few galleons along the way to build this beauty, eh?"

"I assure you, Mr. Teach, no galleons were stolen for

this castle's construction." Headmistress Flora extends her long, slender hand to shake his dirty one. "Welcome to Fairy Tale Reform School. We're thrilled you've decided to join our staff."

He pats his full belly. "Sure. It be time I take a short break from the seas," he says. "Too many be on me tail for me fortune." He winks at Ollie.

"Some of which Mr. Teach has donated to Fairy Tale Reform School's after-school activities," Headmistress Flora says hurriedly. "Children, please meet your new psychology professor, Mr. Edward Teach."

"Flora, don't be so formal!" he says. "I prefer to be called Blackbeard."

"I knew it!" Ollie says, extending his hand to shake Blackbeard's. "It's an honor to meet you, sir. Ollie Funklehouse, from Pete the Cheat's crew."

"Pete the Cheat?" Blackbeard thinks for a moment. "Never heard of him."

"Blackbeard the pirate?" Maxine interrupts, almost stuttering. "But you're…you're…you're…"

"Dangerous?" Blackbeard wipes his nose with the sleeve of his jacket, then lets out a burp so foul I want to run away.

(He doesn't say "excuse me" afterward either.) "Was a bit of a beast before," Blackbeard says, scratching at his beard and hitting some of the beads in the process. "Depends on whom ye ask. But the lovely Madame Cleo over there showed me the error of me ways. Ain't that right, love?" He points to the stunning mermaid I'm used to seeing inside a giant aquarium where she teaches charm classes (and moderates detention). This afternoon she's sunning her scales on a rock.

"Eddie, you're such a love!" Madame Cleo giggles, her tail swishing back and forth as her hair changes from blue to purple to hot pink. "I knew if I visited your ship enough times for a cup of tea, you'd see the error of your pirating ways. And he did," she tells us, taking a starfish from the water to hold her hair in a side ponytail. "His men have seen a total change in him, which is why he makes such an excellent choice to teach students about feelings."

"I didn't think piracy and expressing feelings actually went together," Jax says, and we all look at him in alarm. Is he really questioning the most fearsome pirate Enchantasia—and the world—has ever seen? "No offense," he adds.

Blackbeard stares at my friend before he lets out a loud laugh followed by a burp.

Madame Cleo tsks. "We still have to work on his manners," she mumbles.

Blackbeard claps his meaty hand around Jax's back. "I like this lad! Ye're all right, matey! Are they all this brazen?" Blackbeard asks Flora and Wolfington. "We should get along swimmingly in me classroom. I'm going to run a tight ship."

"It's not your classroom," Jocelyn snaps. "It's my sister's."

"*Was* your sister's," I correct her. "When you plot with a villain to destroy our royal court and try to burn down the school you work for, I assume you lose your right to teach reform school." I look at Jax. "Am I crazy or correct?"

"Correct!" Ollie seconds.

"Miss Gillian, this is neither the time nor the place for this type of behavior!" Headmistress Flora stares at me for a moment. "And since when do you have a purple streak of hair?"

"Gillian Cobbler?" Blackbeard interrupts her. "Yer bravery be legend in these parts. Such courage for a wee lass! Ye must be part pirate!"

"Gilly?" Ollie cries, insulted. "But we all helped save—"

"Maybe I am part pirate!" I wonder aloud, a bit pleased that a pirate as famous as Blackbeard has heard of me. *Wow.*

I'm famous! "I've never been very good at following the rules." Wolfington coughs. "But I've never done anything evil—unlike Harlow."

"That's the Evil Queen you're talking about," Jocelyn says. "Show some respect."

"Don't you mean the *former* Evil Queen?" Jax asks innocently. "I thought Professor Harlow transformed so she could teach here. Oh, that's right!" He claps his hand against his uniform pants. "She was secretly working for the enemy."

Flora tries to intervene. "Children, this is not a conversation we need to bore Mr. Teach with."

"How do we know you aren't still working with her now?" Kayla asks, also ganging up on Jocelyn (which I'm enjoying since it's usually the other way around). "I don't understand why she's still allowed to go here," Kayla says to the headmistress. "She helped her sister capture us!"

Jocelyn's face is purple. "Flora knows my innocence just like she knows Harlow's." Jocelyn appeals to Blackbeard. "Alva tricked her! Harlow is just misunderstood."

I snort. "'Misunderstood' is code for 'prone to be bad.'"

Blackbeard slaps Wolfington on the back. "What a group of scallywags. This be a fun gig! I can tell."

Jocelyn turns her palm upward as a small swirl of purple smoke begins to spiral around her fingers. "Take that back or you'll regret it!"

"Bring it on," I say, courting disaster. "Show our professors why you should be locked up in a dungeon like your sister."

"Illegal use of magic!" I hear Miri's voice and wonder where a mirror is. Oh! I see it on that large oak tree over there, disguised as a squirrel burrow. Smart.

Jocelyn ignores Miri's warning and aims a purple fireball at me. I don't move. If she hits me, it will hurt, but at least Jocelyn will finally be seen as the villain-in-training I know she is.

"Gilly, duck!" Kayla cries in panic, but I won't do it.

Instead, Maxine dives on top of me, knocking me to the ground. We watch as the fireball hits a pirate on the gang-plank who's unloading one of Blackbeard's trunks. The pirate yelps, dropping the trunk in the water.

"Me treasures!" Blackbeard yells.

"I'll get them, darling," says Madame Cleo, giving us a look. "Even if I did just apply a seaweed conditioning treat-ment to my hair." She dives below the water.

"Look what you've done," Jocelyn says. "You're always

thinking of you, you, you! Like you're some hero! You just got lucky."

Madame Cleo pops out of the water with the trunk and hands it off to a pirate who wades into the water. "I think I caught it before anything got wet." She glares at us, her pink hair turning fiery blue. "You children should be ashamed. Failing to listen to your teacher, illegal use of magic, fighting on school grounds. Detention for everyone!"

Blackbeard's laughter is loud and deep. "Not necessary, Madame. This group has spunk. I like it!" He grabs Jocelyn and me by the backs of our uniforms, which I hope rip because I despise these blue jumpers. "Ye two need to get this aggression out. Me thinks a duel will do nicely."

"A duel?" Jocelyn and I say as another cannon blast echoes around us.

"Mr. Teach, I must insist we not have cannon fire on the school grounds." Headmistress Flora sounds like she's losing patience.

"Me men didn't fire, Flora ol' girl." Blackbeard motions to the pirates scurrying by us with trunks and, alarmingly, chests full of weapons. "They all be busy getting me wares to me new quarters. The ship be empty."

KABOOM!

Another cannonball comes whirling toward us, causing Blackbird to drop me and Jocelyn and dive onto the ground with the rest of my teachers and friends and the bewildered pirates.

"Blimey! What be those vile beasts?" Blackbeard asks.

Gargoyles! A whole mess of smelly, winged beasties are suddenly hanging from the ship rafters, climbing the crow's nest, and swinging from the sides of the pirate ship. Their large, scaly wings flutter open and closed as the furry beasts jump up and down and fly around the ship. I hold my breath, waiting to see if they come after us. Those claws mean business.

"Me ship!" Blackbeard cries.

"Take these, sir." Ollie produces a strand of radishes from behind Blackbeard's ear. "They keep the beasties away. One whiff and they'll fall fast asleep."

"Really?" Blackbeard ties the radishes to a bead in his hair.

"We've dealt with them before," says Ollie. "At first, we thought they were statues around school, but then they came alive and we found out they were working for Alva."

And that's when I remember. Where there are gargoyles, there's usually Sleeping Beauty's nightmare in the flesh.

"Alva?" Blackbeard repeats. "You mean that wench?" He points back to the ship. It's as if the wicked fairy has appeared out of thin air.

Sleeping Beauty's nemesis spent ten years pretending to be another villain while she quietly plotted her revenge on the royals—and now she's back. Alva walks to the edge of the plank, her long, red dress billowing in the wind. The collar of her matching red cape reaches the gold clips in her black hair. Alva always looks like she's ready for a ball instead of a brawl. Why villains always wear the same outfits, I'll never know. Alva waves as if she's greeting old friends.

"Miss me, my pets?" Alva cackles in a voice so high-pitched that it makes me want to cover my ears. "I'm back to collect what's rightfully mine."

"Put the school on lockdown," Flora tells Wolfington and Madame Cleo hurriedly. They don't argue. "No one comes out 'til it's safe." Wolfington takes off at wolf speed, while the Sea Siren dives off a rock and into the waters, her shimmery blue-green tail barely visible below the surface. Flora turns to us. "The rest of you, inside. Now."

Kayla appears frozen. "She's here. She's back. She's here."

"She won't touch you. Just get inside." Flora tries to

shepherd us toward the large wooden doors at the back of the castle, while Blackbeard instructs his men where to go. Everyone is shouting; the gargoyles are shrieking; Miri's alarm system is now blaring. Kayla runs for the doors with Maxine, while Ollie begins hurling radishes in the air.

Jax pulls me back and whispers in my ear. "Why aren't the gargoyles flying toward us?" he asks as chaos swirls around us. "If Alva is here to attack the school, wouldn't her gargoyles have come after us by now? Kind of convenient that they had Blackbeard's ship to land on, isn't it?" His violet eyes are thoughtful. "It's as if she knew he'd be here."

The two of us look at each other and without him knowing, I slip my hand into his pocket and take something I may need to borrow. Then I take off at a run.

"Headmistress Flora!" I shout, trying to get her attention as she talks to Miri at the oak tree. "What if Alva's gargoyles are a distraction? What if she's after Harlow?"

At her sister's name, Jocelyn appears at my side. I ignore her.

"*Professor* Harlow, Gillian, and I don't have time for theories," Flora says. "We're under attack."

"But she's not attacking," I point out, pulling on Flora's

petticoat so I can show her. We turn in time to see a gargoyle moving the cannon fire toward a wall near the back of the castle. It blows a hole right through the side of the building.

"What room be that?" Blackbeard asks. "What say ye of casualties?"

"It's a storage area for the kitchen," Flora tells him.

"But aren't the dungeons below the kitchen?" I ask and both Jocelyn and Flora look at me. So does Blackbeard. He glances back at the ship.

"The wench is gone!" He points to where we last saw Alva.

"She's trying to break out the Evil Queen!" I tell Flora, yelling over the sound of more cannon fire aimed at the same place. Another hole is blasted at the same spot, this time opening up the ground. A team of gargoyles flies to the area. "Someone has to check on her!" And by someone, I mean me. I race toward the gargoyles.

"Miss Gillian and Miss Jocelyn, get back here!" Flora yells.

My eyes are on Harlow's little sister, who obviously knew I was right. She's running the same way for a different reason—to help her big sister, I'm sure. We're both so close to the castle that I know if I don't do something to slow Jocelyn down, she'll reach Harlow first.

I pull Jax's pocket watch that I pinched out of my pocket. That's right, I still got it. "*Houratiempo!*" I shout, remembering the strange word I've heard Jax utter before. A light bursts from the watch and sends Jocelyn flying backward. I run toward her, knowing the power of that pocket watch means she can still talk but she can't move for the next few minutes. I slide into her side and tie her hands with the long, purple gingerroot flower stems Maxine plucked for a rainy day.

Found near the edge of the Hollow Woods, the rare electric-blue flower with the purple stems has the power to freeze people temporarily and also to bind them from using magic when the stem is wrapped around their wrists. Ever since Alva threatened me, Maxine has insisted that I have gingerroot in my pocket at all times. It came in handy today.

"Gilly, let go!" Jocelyn screams. Since I only tied the roots around her wrists, her lungs still work.

"You're not escaping with Harlow," I say. "You—"

BOOM! Pieces of the castle wall explode in the air, sending rocks and debris raining down on us. I can't hear anything but ringing. My right leg is pinned under a piece of wall. Jocelyn is stuck under a fallen wooden door. When the smoke clears, I see two figures approaching. One slaps a long, hand-written scroll that glows on a crumbling wall before walking my way. A sinister smile plays on the woman's ruby-red lips.

"Gillian Cobbler," Alva purrs. "Always trying to be the hero. For that you'll pay dearly." I see her lift her hand.

"*No!*" Harlow shouts. "Leave the brats! We must go!" Harlow pulls Alva away.

"Harlow, listen!" Jocelyn screams, but the Evil Queen doesn't stop.

For a brief moment, the two of us lock eyes. Then Harlow and Alva disappear in a cloud of smoke.

Happily Ever After Scrolls

Brought to you by FairyWeb—magically appearing on scrolls throughout Enchantasia for the past ten years!

BREAKING NEWS:

Alva at FTRS! Breaks Evil Queen Out of Dungeon! Releases Villainous Call to Arms!

by Beatrice Beez

Yesterday afternoon, Enchantasia's most-wanted villain appeared on Fairy Tale Reform School grounds where she broke the Evil Queen out of captivity and the two escaped under the noses of FTRS teachers. To make matters worse, *HEAS* has learned that Alva left a villainous manifesto at the school. The call to arms supposedly promises greater riches than the 10,000 gold pieces the Dwarf Police Squad is offering as a reward for Alva's capture and encourages students to join Alva and Harlow in taking over Enchantasia and destroying the royal court of Princesses Ella, Snow White, Rapunzel, and our Sleeping Beauty, Rose.

Miri the FTRS spokesmirror would not allow *HEAS*

to see the manifesto, which is being examined by the Dwarf Police Squad. "Our teachers will not indulge Alva's deluded request by sharing it with the public," says Miri. "Headmistress Flora has addressed the students about Alva's message and used the scroll to reinforce the school motto—being bad brings about no good. We will not lose our students to villainy. Our goal remains the same: to help our students reform and follow the straight and narrow path."

Parents of students at FTRS are still understandably concerned. What did Alva's message actually say, and could it sway their children to join the dark side? "How long can we allow our children to remain in FTRS's care when these former villains obviously can't keep them safe?" asks Millicent Gertrude, the mother of Ronald Gertrude, who is in FTRS for six months for the illegal trading of Pegasi. "Constant break-ins, castle explosions, calls to villainy— what is going on there? I want visitation day moved up so I can see for myself if my Porridge Bottom is safe."

"We take our school's security very seriously," says Miri. "At this time, we are looking at our schedule to see whether visitation day can be moved up. But parents should know all the students in our care are safe." For now FTRS plans to host its semiannual parent visitation in a few weeks. Many villagers are excited to meet Princess Rose, who has taken on a consulting gig with the school to shepherd their famed Royal Ladies-in-Waiting Club. "I love the idea of helping the next generation of girls put their best glass slipper forward," said Rose when reached for comment.

Keep checking HEAS for updates on the search for the wicked fairy and the Evil Queen and their villainous manifesto!

CHAPTER 3

Cordially Invited

We're not supposed to be here.

This area of the castle was forbidden *before* Alva's gargoyles blew a hole in it and destroyed the kitchen storage closet. (When you go to school with hungry ogres, locking up food is essential.) But today the bombed-out wall of the castle is cordoned off by glowing Dwarf Police Squad caution tape.

Please. Like yellow tape is going to keep a bunch of reform-school students from reading a villain's manifesto.

The large, yellowed scroll hangs on a crumbling piece of wall by magic rather than a nail. That explains why the Dwarf Police Squad's Pete and Olaf made ineffective, and comical, attempts to remove the scroll. Alva obviously bewitched her credo so that it can't come down. Despite our teachers' lecture yesterday afternoon about Alva and what a danger she is to not only FTRS, but Enchantasia, every kid I know still wants to hear what she has to say…including me.

I inch closer to the wall to read Alva's warning. I'm not usually so nervous, but I guess I have a lot more to lose these days. In my brother Felix's last Pegasus Post, he told me that thanks to Father making glass slippers again, my siblings are all eating three meals a day. They also have new clothes and warm blankets for their joint bed. I don't want to do anything to jeopardize that. And yet, I'm still sneaking over to read the manifesto. We crowd around the glowing, golden scroll to read the large, loopy, red scrolled handwriting.

Students of Fairy Tale Reform School

You've been warned: Enchantasia will be no more!

Soon the Evil Queen and I will rule this kingdom! Whose side will you be on when that
day comes?

If you're in FTRS, then you know how to
be wicked, and being wicked is smart in this
day and age.

Interested? Just make your intentions known,
children, and we'll hear your pleas. We'll be
back to claim you before you know it, and
I promise that measly reward of 10,000
gold pieces for my capture is nothing compared to the fortune you'll get with me.
Alva

"You have to admit, posting a call to evil at Fairy Tale Reform
School is brilliant," I say as we jostle for position around the
scroll. It's hard when students are pushing and conjuring small
spells to move others out of the way. "If you need to build a
wicked army, what better place to find one than here?"

"No wonder Flora seemed so wound up." Jax plants his legs wide to keep from being knocked down and losing his place in front of the scroll. "She was so busy getting ready for the school lecture on evil that she barely reprimanded you and Jocelyn about taking off after Alva."

I elbow the ogre behind me for kneeing me in the back. "Maybe, but that didn't stop her from repeating her classic line, 'I'd hate for you to add more time to your sentence here at FTRS.' And instead of detention with Madame Cleo, she said something about Jocelyn and I having to duel in Blackbeard's class today. She can't mean a *real* duel, can she?"

"Yes!" Jax nudges me, probably by accident since we're being pushed around. "Flora might be the only one around here not impressed by your new hero title."

"Hero?" I sputter. I've never heard Jax use that word about me before. Sure, *Happily Ever After Scrolls* and unnamed sources keep calling me one, but never my friends. Wouldn't anyone do what I did to stay alive and help their school? I'd hope so, but if being a hero is what keeps my family well fed, then I'm not going to argue. "Anyone would do what we did."

Jax frowns as his finger traces Alva's loopy letter *A*. "Not everyone would stick their necks out for a royal," he teases, and I make a face. Jax is the only royal I like, and he knows it. "Too bad we didn't catch Alva though. She's not going to stop until she controls Enchantasia."

I stare at the manifesto again. "What do you think she means by 'make your intentions known and we'll hear your plea'?"

Jax pushes his floppy curls out of his eyes. "I don't know." He pulls me away from the scroll, and kids quickly press into the empty spot. "What if she means the mole and that mole is at Fairy Tale Reform School?"

The whole reason Jax is undercover at FTRS is to find the mole that is trying to tear apart the royal court. His dad thought Jax would have luck getting the scoop at a school where the kids know every dirty trick in *Evildoing for Dummies*. So far though, we've had no luck. This mole, whoever he may be, is still feeding villains info on the princesses and now seems close enough to get into our school. I feel a shiver race through me.

"What if the mole is helping Alva because he or she hates the royal court *and* wants power?" I wonder. A group of pixies fly by our heads and I pause. They whisper and point when they see me. "The kids in here could help Alva a lot. They're likely to be the next big-time villains if they don't reform. And a lot of them have magic!"

"We'll hear your plea." Jax repeats a line from the scroll. "The mole *must* be at FTRS. How else could Alva reach the students or know Blackbeard was coming, giving her time to break out Harlow?" We step over crumbling bricks to exit the kitchen storage room and walk onto the lawn outside the school. Jax's brow is wrinkled in concentration. "This doesn't add up. Wouldn't Flora have worried about Harlow as soon as she saw Alva? Instead, she ignored you when you tried to warn her."

Warning bells go off in my head. I've thought the worst of our school headmistress before. *Once a villain, always part villain*, I've heard Wolfington say. Could it be true? Could Flora have helped Harlow break out? Why? And if she did, how do we stop Flora and this mole from striking again?

A shadow crosses over Jax's face and we both look up. A group of magic carpets flies by with student drivers. The carpets are an array of bright purples, blues, pinks, and brilliant oranges, with tassels hanging so low that one brushes my head. The patterns are as varied as the colors. In your first magic carpet class, you actually get to design your own carpet: color, pattern, aerodynamics, and special effects. A shower of glitter rains down on Jax and me like snow.

"Miss Hobby, we are not glittering the castle today!" Monsieur Lavine scolds. "It's not a holiday! Helmut, we fly behind one other, not one on top of the other." Our teacher looks down and spots us. He removes his silver turban and tosses it to Jax. "A little late to class, are we, Mr. Jax? Meet us at the Pegasi stables, and as punishment, you must wear my turban for the rest of the day." His classmates laugh as Jax places the large, oversized silver hat on his head. The jewels hanging off it make it hard for him to see.

"Great," Jax grumbles, and the jewels in front of his eyes sway. "As if Ollie wasn't already giving me grief about being a royal, now I'm a royal wearing noble headgear. I've got to go. Talk later?"

He looks so glum that I resist the urge to poke fun at his royalness. The ground shakes and I look up. Maxine is bounding toward me.

"Hey! Why was Jax in a turban?" she asks breathlessly. "No matter. Did you guys read the manifesto? Scary, huh? Alva's trying to take over our school!" She clutches one of the dozens of pearl necklaces stretched around her thick neck. "My scroll sent me another message about it this morning."

I sigh. "Maxine, mini magical scrolls don't send messages. You must just—"

Maxine thrusts her scroll into my face. "Look! At the bottom. That's not *Happily Ever After Scrolls*'s writing. It says 'She'll be back. She's gaining numbers. Watch that those around you don't fall for her thunder.'" Her one eye rolls quickly in its socket.

"I…" I stare closer. The handwriting *is* different and the writing glows blue, while the rest of the *HEAS* message is in black. But it can't be. Not to be rude, but why would someone use Maxine to stop Alva? "Let me know if this happens again, okay?"

Maxine nods. "There's more. Mama sent a Pegasus Post this morning, and she said if the break-ins continue, she might talk to Headmistress Flora about pulling me out of school." Her large hand clasps mine. "Is it weird that I don't want to go home yet?" she whispers. "I kind of like it here. I finally have friends."

I smile. A group of Pegasi neigh as they fly by us with more student riders. Out on the lawn, I see a bunch of kids in full armor starting dragon training against a mechanical dragon that shoots real fire. I miss my family, but there are things at Fairy Tale Reform School that I'd never get to do in the real world. I squeeze Maxine's large hand. "I know what you mean. Don't worry about it right now. Let's get to class." We step back inside the crumbling kitchen storage room just as the closest mirror begins to glow orange, purple, then turquoise green.

"This area of the castle is off-limits!" Miri announces, and her decree is followed by groans. "Students seen in this area in the next two minutes will spend the next three days in detention with Madame Cleo or Blackbeard. I should warn you that he's teaching duels." Kids disperse immediately, and Maxine and I jump into a new hallway appearing to our left. Kayla is waiting.

"Hey," she says when she sees us. "Why weren't you in our room this morning?" I watch her wings pop in and out over and over, which only happens when she's nervous. "You didn't want to have breakfast together?"

Kayla and I are roomies, but ever since I found out she was secretly working with Alva—whether she was black-mailed into doing it or not—things have been, shall we say, a bit off between us. "I had to meet with Flora about Jocelyn,"

I say, which is only partly a lie. I met with Flora, but I had cinnamon rolls for breakfast with Jax first.

"Oh, okay." Kayla still looks disappointed. "Did you tell Flora you think Jocelyn was working with Harlow to escape? Because I'm sure she was."

"I was too busy trying to convince Flora that Jocelyn wanted to escape with Harlow." We walk by enchanted classroom doors that seal shut when all the students are inside. It's a new safety measure since Alva's last break-in. "Jocelyn said I'm lying, and Flora foolishly believed her." I sigh. "Bottom line: Flora says Alva's the one who broke Harlow out, not Jocelyn. Jocelyn seemed upset she was left behind."

"I feel kind of bad for her being abandoned like that." Maxine's good eye widens. "Oh, I just meant... I..."

"It's fine. Forget it," Kayla says, and Maxine and I look at each other. Kayla wasn't exactly abandoned. Her whole family was cursed by Alva and turned into a group of trees. Still, Maxine's comment had to sting. "I should go," she says and flutters away. She's barely gone a few feet before the hallway mirror glows purple.

"Illegal use of magic, Kayla!" Miri reprimands her. "No flying in the hallways!"

Kayla ignores her. "So? Give me detention. I'm not leaving this place anytime soon."

Maxine shakes her head. "That fairy needs a pick-me-up." Her good eye widens. "I know! We should do a girl day and paint our nails or visit mermaids at the lake or... Ooh! Let's join the Royal Ladies-in-Waiting together. It would be fun to be in a club, wouldn't it?"

"Not the RLWs!" I say quickly, not that the other options are more appealing. Painting nails? Hanging with mermaids? I'd rather be baked in an oven. "Maybe we could do fencing." A hallway disappears and we take the new one to the left. Thankfully it pops out on the lower level where we need to be. We have our first group therapy class with Blackbeard down here.

"Gillian Cobbler?"

I turn around and my shoulders sink. A gaggle of Royal Ladies-in-Waiting are staring at me. You can tell they're in the FTRS club because they wear bright-pink sashes over their school uniforms and always have creepy smiles plastered on their picture-perfect faces. I wonder if they heard me talking to Maxine.

A goblin named Tessa Underlin steps forward and holds out a cream-colored envelope wrapped in a bright-pink ribbon. She's the RLW president, and she's wearing a tiara and a glittery, jeweled necklace. Her pointy ears are adorned with earrings much like Maxine wears. "We'd like to present you with an invitation to join the Royal Ladies-in-Waiting."

"Oh, Gilly!" Maxine cries, smacking her heart as I stare at the pink-and-gold lettering on the thick envelope. "You're so lucky!"

Tessa barely looks at Maxine, but I notice that the others start to whisper.

"You are the sole member we are recruiting for the club this semester, and we'd be ever so pleased if you could join us on our royal journey," Tessa adds.

"Recruit?" I repeat. "I thought clubs at FTRS were open to all students."

Tessa smiles smugly. I notice the pink patches on her uniform sash. She has more than any of the other girls, and I suspect it's because she's earned the most badges. All the girls start with the same five: a glass slipper, a wand, a hairbrush, a tube of lipstick, and a tiara. "We are exclusive, and we only accept members who meet our proper lady criteria."

"*I* meet your criteria?" I notice a chocolate stain on my skirt. "I am not a lady."

For a second Tessa looks at me like I'm a bitter biscuit. "You are a hero and that gives you a certain status. Princess Rose, our new advisor, asked for you personally. Princesses have endured so much that we commoners have not," she gushes. "You've faced evil and survived, just like them. That makes you Royal Lady-in-Waiting material." The girls behind her nod their heads in agreement.

I frown. "I don't see it. I'm sure you guys never get your hands dirty."

Tessa looks uncomfortable. "We're learning. With Alva's call to arms, we have to be ready for anything."

My villain radar goes up. "You guys have read the manifesto?"

"Of course," says a pixie sitting on another member's shoulder. "Princess Rose held an emergency discussion on evil and power just last night that we all attended."

"So?" Tessa presses. "I assume you're interested. No one turns down Princess Rose. She's tough. She says it's never too early for a lady to learn how to defend herself."

I find that sentiment surprising coming from a royal. "Why not just let a dashing prince come to your rescue instead?" I crack myself up, the sound echoing through the hall. No one else laughs. I stare at the stained glass window above me, wishing I had a way to climb up it and disappear.

"Princess Rose says you can't wait for someone else to do the rescuing," Tessa says tartly. "If Royal Ladies-in-Waiting want something, they have to grab it."

Like ruling Enchantasia? Could one of these princess wannabes secretly be working with Alva? I glance at Maxine, trying to somehow tell her what I'm thinking, but she's still drooling—literally—over Tessa's jewelry. Maybe if I went to an RLW meeting, I could find out if the mole is among them. That's what a hero would do, right?

Hmm…but do I really want to go to a club meeting where everything is pink? *Shudder.* I tug at my brown hair, which I never even combed this morning. "I'll check out a meeting if Maxine can come with me," I say. "She is just as much a potential Royal Lady-in-Waiting as I am."

Tessa looks at Maxine's lumpy frame and winces. "Maxine?"

I put my arm around Maxine. At least I try to. She's much bigger than me. "She's been helping out at your events all year."

Tessa looks at the others. "But…well…you see, we have very strict criteria."

"Last time she tried to help, she crushed the flowers with her pudgy hand!" cries one royal wannabe with a particularly crooked nose.

"I did," Maxine admits, her right eye rolling madly.

"She makes a mess when she's eating, and her food flew into my mouth one time!" says a girl whose hair is so bright red I think it might be made of flames.

"I am kind of sloppy." Maxine burps for added benefit. The girls giggle.

I've had enough. I shove my invitation back into Tessa's hands.

"If you guys don't think Maxine is RLW material, then you're not the kind of girls I want to hang out with," I say indignantly. How could girls who are this obsessed with princesses have a member who's the mole? I take back my original idea. Who needs them?

The final bell chimes, and students duck and roll through the closing classroom door. I have to make it through before it seals shut and I get extra detention time with Madame Cleo. Where I'd have to do dance lessons. *Shudder.*

"But Princess Rose…" Tessa starts to say.

"You can tell Princess Rose that if she wants me to be in

her royal-lover club, she'll put Maxine in it as well," I say.

"Okay! We will!" Tessa calls after me as I race to the classroom door. "And by the way, love the purple stripe in your hair!"

Grr... I pull Maxine with me as we dive through the doorway to Professor Harlow's—I mean Blackbeard's—classroom before the door seals shut with a slurp.

"Ah, the other lass we've been looking for!" Blackbeard says.

I look up and my jaw drops. Where the heck am I?

Blackbeard puts a strong hand on my shoulder and leads me to the front of the classroom where a pouty Jocelyn is waiting. He flashes a mouth of rotten teeth. "Ready for your duel, poppet?"

Happily Ever After Scrolls
Brought to you by FairyWeb—magically appearing on scrolls throughout Enchantasia for the past ten years!

Meet Fairy Tale Reform School's New Teacher: Blackbeard the Pirate!

by Coco Collette

Name: Edward Teach but he's better known as Blackbeard for his famed long, black beard beaded with jewels from the Orient.

Former Occupation: "Pillaging, plundering, and having lots of jolly good fun!" says Blackbeard, who was more than happy to sit down for an interview with *HEAS*.

Current Occupation: "Teaching lads and lasses how to swab the decks." (We translated this to mean: "Clean up thar acts.")

Hobbies: Fencing. Blackbeard is taking over Professor Harlow's role as fencing team coach. The former pirate also enjoys "a good sea chantey, and Madame Cleo knows plenty of them." (Hmm…makes us wonder about those romance rumors.)

Strengths: Fear tactics. In battle, Blackbeard was a

menacing sight. He dressed in black and tied fuses to his hair so they'd give off smoke. Enemies would surrender on sight. "It's about the illusion, matey!" No idea how this tactic will go over in a classroom.

Weaknesses: "I've been swayed by a bonny lass before." Paging Madame Cleo...

Likes: Captaining a ship, the smell of sea air, and intellectual ARRguments

Hates: Insubordination. "If ye don't follow me rules, I'll make ye walk the plank!"

Check back for more coverage on FTRS's newest teacher, Blackbeard the Pirate!

CHAPTER 4

Captain of the Ship

∿

Professor Harlow's room has been completely transformed overnight. It looks like the deck of what I assume is a pirate ship. Where the Evil Queen's desk once stood is now a helm with a wooden ship's wheel, and nearby, sails and ropes ascend to the ceiling. The floor beneath my feet is made of wooden planks that are being swabbed by a pirate. Another pirate is dusting a large, wooden serpent statue that I recognize from the bow of Blackbeard's ship. He must have moved it into his new classroom, right behind the mock ship's wheel.

At the far end of the classroom, or deck, are our old desks and the mer-folk tanks, which are now decorated with sea creatures and netting. The only thing I recognize is Miri's mirror hanging on a door to nowhere. The room used to be so dark you could barely see your quill, but now the walls beyond the ship's deck are enchanted to look like a sea. It's calm and the sun is shining, but in the distance I can see storm clouds rolling in.

"Crew!" Blackbeard says to the class as Jocelyn and I stand next to him. "We will start our first lesson with a duel between..." Blackbeard scratches his beard. "Poppets, what are yer names again?"

"Gilly," I say, and the class erupts in cheers. The mer-folk do backflips in their tanks, and the pixies and fairies shoot off mini-fireworks even though they're technically not allowed. Ollie gives me a loud wolf whistle. *Wow. Maybe this hero stuff has its benefits.*

"And ye, love?" Blackbeard motions to my opponent.

"Jocelyn," she says, and you could hear a pin drop.

"Ye rules of dueling arrgh simple." Blackbeard walks to the edge of the ship to grab two swords from a bucket. I feel my stomach drop. The sheen of the blade, the clinking noise the two swords make when he hits them together... Those babies are real! A pixie in the first row starts to whimper.

"Sir!" Maxine waves her arms wildly. "Are those real? Isn't that dangerous?"

Blackbeard laughs. "Of course they're real!" He uses one sword to slice a sail line, which falls on a mer-folk tank. "But don't worry, dearie. Madame Cleo bewitched these beauties so that they can cut everything but people. See?" He uses the sword to nick his own arm and everyone in the room screams. But when he removes his sword, the only thing sliced is his jacket. I breathe a sigh of relief.

"But gettin' cut in battle isn't what ye have to fear, me buckaroos." Blackbeard points to his noggin. "Fear is what ye make of it. If losing is all ye fear, then ye will fight to the death to win!" His voice booms. "If ye battle for another reason—anger, resentment, love—ye have much more to lose, don't ye?" He points to Jocelyn and me with the blade. "What is sending ye into battle this morn?"

Who knew a pirate would make much more sense than an evil queen? Why do I always fight with Jocelyn? I look at her and she stares back at me, her eyes dark as coal. It's because I don't trust villains. Sure, I may sort of be one for my thieving, but that's nothing compared to what she's done. Jocelyn is an evil bully, and I don't like her.

Miri's mirror begins to glow, washing the makeshift pirate ship in a blue that mimics the reflection of the ocean.

"Professor Blackbeard?" Miri's voice comes into the room. "Headmistress Flora would like to have a word in the hall. It's urgent."

Blackbeard removes his hat. "Aargh! Fine." He looks at us. "Ye behave. I'll be out thar."

As soon as he leaves, the room erupts in conversations. Jocelyn moves to the plank at one end of the ship, while I attempt to pen a note to my sister Anna. She's still mad at me for being stuck at FTRS, but I'm hoping eventually she'll send me a Pegasus Post back. I sit down to write and am surprised when a group of students mobs me.

"You've got to beat Jocelyn," says a goblin boy. "We can't stand her." The others nod. "But you'll win! Anyone who went after Alva twice has to."

"Pummel the witch!" someone shouts. It's Ronald Gertrude, this weaselly kid who follows Ollie around. With a pale, pudgy face, eyes like slits, and greasy hair always slicked back in a ponytail, he looks like one of Ella's coachmen who are always pushing villagers off the carriage when it is parked in the square. Rumor has it Ronald is in FTRS for stealing Pegasi, and Maxine heard he's banned from our stables for teasing the animals. I ignore him.

"Jocelyn is no match for you," says a sprite with bright-blue hair. This is the same girl who ran from Jocelyn just a few weeks ago during detention. "No one beats a hero!"

There's that word again. *Hero.* I could get used to that.

"My mom said I could order a pair of your father's glass slippers," says an RLW with a pink bow on her head. "All the princesses have them, but your father can't keep up with orders. Could you, um, maybe put in a call for me?"

"My father says your father is being invited to all the village parties because of how you helped when Alva attacked the school," says a pixie who lands on my shoulder. "Everyone wants to hang out with the Cobblers now."

I smile to myself, thinking of my family being in demand instead of shunned for a change. I wonder if the attention makes Anna happy. Maybe all the village goodwill will make her finally forgive me.

"I was talking to Gilly!" the RLW snaps. Then she smiles at me. "So about the slippers. Can you put in a call for me? Because I really need them ASAP."

Everyone is talking over one other. Maxine is jumping around in the background trying to reach me, but I'm distracted. I never got attention like this at home. Father was disappointed in my thieving, and I was always in trouble. But if sales are as good as this girl and Felix says they are, he must be thrilled. I know I am. I've never had so many people calling my name before, let alone cheering me on. It feels good to be appreciated. I hold my hand up in solidarity and they go nuts. *Holy gingerbread. This is cool.*

"Gilly!" Maxine tries yelling, but I am sure whatever she has to tell me can wait.

"I'm back, buckos!" hollers Blackbeard, and everyone runs to their seats. "We're going to have to cut class early so let's get this duel started. Have ye lasses thought about what I said?" Blackbeard goes to his wheel and gives it a little spin. "So many buccaneers could have spared their lives if they'd just hashed things out without a weapon. Do ye two want to do the same?"

"No," Jocelyn and I say at the same time, and my classmates get excited. I side-eye Maxine. She's too busy talking to Ollie to look at me. Geez, are my friends going to pay attention to my duel?

"Very well, let the dueling begin. Crew, be still." I don't understand what he means 'til Blackbeard points his compass at the back of the room and *bam*! The desks and fish tanks have been moved to the corners of the room—ship…whatever. In their place is a large, flat deck perfect for fencing. "I assume ye both have dueled before?"

"I'm the best fencer on my sister's fencing team," Jocelyn brags.

"Ah, I forgot to mention that." Blackbeard slaps his thigh. "Harlow's out as coach and this buckaroo is in." Jocelyn's eyes look like they're going to bulge out of her head. "Tryouts for ye fencing club be soon!"

"I am so making the team," I boast to Blackbeard. "The Evil Queen isn't here to hold me back." Jocelyn's nostrils flare. I'm enjoying getting a rise out of her. My classmates are applauding, and a warm feeling is spreading through my chest.

"You'll totally make the team, Gilly!" someone yells.

"The only sword you've ever used is a fire poker, Cobbler," Jocelyn snaps. "You think that purple stripe in your hair is a curse? Just wait 'til you slip up. Your school will get destroyed while you're busy stroking your own ego." The class is cheering so loudly that I can barely hear her.

"What did you say?" I move closer, but Blackbeard hands us our swords.

I feel the weight of the steel in my hand. It's not like I

haven't used a sword before. My dagger saved Princess Snow. I'm sure I can manage a proper fight with a sword. I've wanted to be a fencer forever.

"Now take three paces away from each other, and when I give the command, ye will have five minutes on my clock to duel," Blackbeard explains. "Winner gets… What are ye even fighting over?"

I feel my hatred sear. "I want Jocelyn put in the dungeon where she belongs." The class cheers.

"I want Cobbler to keep her peasant nose out of my business." Jocelyn's black cape billows out behind her in a wind that appears out of nowhere.

Blackbeard scratches his beard. "Blimey! I'm not sure I can have anyone locked away or keep ye apart, but we'll come up with something. A little time in the dungeons might suffice. Now walk—and keep it clean, poppets!"

Jocelyn and I turn away from each other as the class cheers us on. I walk three paces and wait 'til I hear Blackbeard give the command. As I do, Ollie bolts for the door and leaves without telling our professor.

"Duel!" Blackbeard commands.

I don't turn at first. I glance Jocelyn's way out of the

corner of my eye with my head down (a great thief technique) so that she can't see me looking. I wait a second, hoping Jocelyn charges and I can jump out of her way, but she's gone. Where'd she go?

Boom!

Jocelyn appears in front of me with glowing eyes. Within seconds, my body flies backward, smacking into a pixie and knocking her into Maxine's hands.

"Fight clean!" Blackbeard bellows as my classmates boo.

"I knew you couldn't fence," Jocelyn says icily and flicks that annoying cape of hers as she makes her way over to where I lie. She raises her sword to strike me.

"And you think you can? You're just using magic," I say, stalling for time until I can figure out my move. Jocelyn's sword comes down over her head to pierce my arm and I roll out of the way. Everyone cheers as I jump up and raise my own sword.

"Look at you and your cheering section," Jocelyn mocks.

"Jealous?" I ask, slicing a hole in a star on her cape.

"Never!" she says. "Being popular doesn't make you better. And at least I don't have purple hair."

The two of us clink swords across the ship-classroom

toward Blackbeard, who watches quietly. *Clink! Rattle! Clink!* I swipe one way, then the other, and then our swords connect above our heads. I may not be on the fencing team, but that doesn't mean I haven't practiced. Jocelyn doesn't realize I have three little brothers who spend most of their waking hours pretending to be pirates.

I'm closing in on Jocelyn, inching her toward the side of the ship, when I see her whisper an incantation. I'm knocked on my back again. This time, I'm not going quietly.

I've got tricks too. I may be on the ground, but Jocelyn's cape is so large that I can grab a handful of it and yank. Jocelyn goes flying. "I always knew your cape was trouble."

"I'll give you trouble." Jocelyn starts swirling her right wrist like she's stirring hot cocoa with a spoon. A purple haze begins to spin up from the floor. I may not have magic at my fingertips, but I'm smarter than she is. I spot the sail line hanging next to me, grab one end, and cut the other from its attached sandbag. The rope sends me flying above the classroom into the rafters above, and I pull myself up onto a wooden beam.

Jocelyn attempts to follow me, but as she's on her way up, I cut her line, sending her falling down to the floor again. *Yes!*

As the kids cheer, I grab another rope and begin to shimmy down when—*Aaah!* Jocelyn's cut my line.

I'm falling, falling, falling. I hear people screaming, and the ground flying up to meet me, but I can do nothing to stop myself. I put my hands in front of my face to brace myself and feel my body snap like a rubber band. When I open one eye, I realize I've stopped inches from the ground and am floating there. I look over and see Jocelyn in the middle of a spell meant for me. Her conjuring has kept me from smacking into the floor.

"Looks like you owe me, Cobbler." Jocelyn taunts and any chance of me thanking her goes out the window. "Good!" She drops me the few inches to the floor. "I guess I really do control you now."

Jocelyn has gone too far. I spring up and race at her with my sword raised high. Her eyes widen and she steps back, preparing for us to clink blades. *Clink! Clink! Clink!* We go back and forth, around and around, faster this time. The crowd is cheering again and chanting my name. *Gilly! Gilly! Gilly!* I love the sound of them saying it while Jocelyn strains to keep up with me. She looks nervous. She should be! I can't disappoint my fans—I have to win this duel.

So I cheat.

While Jocelyn's sword is raised, I use my free hand to grab her hair and yank.

"*Ouch!*" She turns around and pulls my purple locks of hair. Both of us drop our swords and pounce, rolling to the ground and doing what we started to do the other day—fighting the good, old-fashioned way. I mean, the *other* old-fashioned way. With name-calling and hair-pulling.

"Liar!" I cry.

"Thief!" Jocelyn bellows.

"Wicked!" I taunt.

"Cobbler!" Jocelyn sputters. "Poor man's daughter!"

My blood is ready to boil over. "Why couldn't you have just disappeared along with your sister?" I shout. "I know! Because she didn't want you! She left you behind on purpose!" Jocelyn stops fighting.

I see Jocelyn's pained reaction just as we disappear under a sail that's been dropped onto us. The sail pulls us close, rolling us up. Within seconds, we're both mummified.

"Time!" Blackbeard yells through the wrapping.

The world around us is eerily quiet. We're lying on top of each other, and the only sound I hear is Jocelyn's and my breath going in and out. I hesitate, feeling slightly guilty, but I'm still unsure of what I want to say. "Jocelyn, I…"

She snaps her fingers and we unravel, me rolling into a wall.

"It seems ye be tied!" Blackbeard says.

My classmates are cheering, but Maxine looks horrified.

"It's not a tie." Jocelyn staggers toward me, straightening out her crooked robe. "The *hero* won. At least that's what everyone here is going to say." She looks straight at me. "Just remember—the bigger the hero is, the harder they fall." Her eyes flash purple. "And I can't wait to be here when you go splat." Then in the purple haze I've become accustomed to, Jocelyn snaps her fingers and disappears.

Pegasus Postal Service

Flying Letters Since The Troll War!

FROM: Gillian Cobbler (Fairy Tale Reform School*)

*Letter checked for suspicious content

TO: Anna Cobbler (2 Boot Way)

Anna Banana,

You are even harder to reach than the royals! This is the fourth post I've sent this month. Every one gets returned to sender. Did you move to a new boot and not tell me?

If you haven't moved, and you really are my sister, Anna Cobbler of 2 Boot Way, then hear me out. I'm sorry, okay? I stayed here to protect you. I want you, Felix, Trixie, Han, and Hamish to be safe. I want Father's boot business to continue to do well. I want Mother to have time off to read a book or put her feet up on the sofa. (Not that she ever will. She hates shoes on furniture!)

Felix wrote and said getting Father's glass-slipper gig back has helped a ton with money and meals. I'm glad! If me being a hero helps our family, then I'm happy I'm stuck at FTRS. I'd do anything for you. I hope you know that.

My roommate says visitation day is going to get moved up. I really hope you'll consider coming with Father and Mother to see me. I miss you more than you know.

Love, Gilly Bean

Happily Ever After Scrolls

Brought to you by FairyWeb—magically appearing on scrolls throughout Enchantasia for the past ten years!

Meet the Teacher: Our Very Own Princess Rose Is Working at FTRS!

by Coco Collette

Name: Princess Rose, a.k.a. Sleeping Beauty, who escaped Alva's slumbering curse

Dual Occupations!

The Princess: "I love my kingdom and having the chance to mingle with my people, but one wishes to be seen as more than just a crown."

The Club Advisor: Running the distinguished Royal Ladies-in-Waiting. The RLWs have served at kingdom dinners, decorated carriages for public rides, and have been known to go glass-slipper shopping for their princesses. "With proper training, every girl can be charming enough to find the princess within."

Hobbies: Dancing (she won the royal dance-off five years in a row), singing (she leads the royal a cappella group), and...hunting? "I find it keeps me focused."

Strengths: While the other princesses handle politics, crime, and public policy, Rose is a princess of the public. "I know what my kingdom needs because I spend so much time among the people. That's why I am so impressed with Gillian Cobbler. This hero rose from humble beginnings. She is more of a lady than most women I know."

Weaknesses: Spinning wheels, of course, and all flowers, except roses, naturally. (As villagers will recall, the thorny gingerroot was found surrounding the room where the princess took her hundred-year slumber. That's enough to turn anyone off flowers!)

Check back for more coverage on FTRS's newest teacher, Princess Rose!

CHAPTER 5

The Conquering Hero

G illy! Gilly! Gilly!"

My classmates carry me out of Blackbeard's room on their shoulders. People are chanting my name and applauding at such an ear-deafening decibel that it feels like I've defeated Alva herself. So this is what it's like to be a hero! I see why the princesses like it—not that I like the princesses now or anything. I just don't get why villains like being evil so much. Being popular is so much better!

"Thanks, everyone," I say as the trolls put me down. They're still cheering. Are Maxine and Ollie seeing this? Where'd they go? "I have to get to my next class." *Groan.* "But I'll see you all at lunch." They cheer some more, and I smile. This is great! A hallway shifts in front of me, and I dash toward it. I land with a thud in a new hall where Jax, Kayla, Ollie, and Maxine have congregated. I roll to a stop on Maxine's big toe.

"*Ouch!*" She hops up and down, making the lanterns above us sway.

"Sorry!" I stand up and brush myself off. They're all looking at me like I'm a stranger. "Where'd you guys go? Did you see me beat Jocelyn? It was amazing! She totally crumbled." Their faces are blank. "What's wrong?"

"There's been an attack on Royal Manor," Kayla explains. "Alva sent her gargoyles to tear things up."

"I tried to tell you in class, but you were being carried off on someone's shoulders," Maxine says.

"Is everyone okay?" I brush off my stockings, which now have a hole in them. That's the third pair I've ruined this month.

"The royal court is fine," Jax says. "Alva somehow knew the guards were away on a training mission while Rapunzel was hosting a tea with the ogre tribes to broker peace. The gargoyles swooped in and scared the ogres off before any progress was made. You know how much they fear beasties."

"Oh, I know," says Maxine, who shudders. "I still have nightmares about the gargoyles' breath."

"How'd you find out so fast?" I ask.

"Father sent me a message with this." Jax pulls a quill out of his pocket. It's one of the magic quills that self-writes a message when you touch the point of the quill to parchment. When you write back with it, the ink disappears so the note can't be confiscated. It's brilliant. I had no idea it could work sending a message as far away as the royal castle. If that's the case, maybe I can get one to Anna.

"Rapunzel got knocked out when she tried to fight the gargoyles off," Jax says. "When she awoke, she found a scroll in her hands with a message." Jax writes something, and Alva's loopy handwriting appears, having been copied by Jax's father. The words give me chills:

You can run, but you can't hide. Nowhere is safe. My ranks are rising, and my power is growing. You've been warned.

"Wow, that villain has a vendetta all right." Ollie shakes his head. "I guess when your evil scheme to curse a princess to sleep fails, you go to the next best plan—take over the whole kingdom."

"Thank goodness Rapunzel is okay." Maxine's love of princesses is legendary.

"My sister is fine, thankfully, but she and Father are really worried," Jax says. "If Alva learns about more peace talks and keeps sending her gargoyles, it could ruin future negotiations. The princesses are *this close* to a treaty. If Alva stops the peace talks, it could mean war."

"No!" Maxine cries. "We ogres have come so far for our freedom. We're finally allowed in the village and at this school. I couldn't even go to FTRS when it first opened. We can't let Alva destroy that."

I put a hand on her shoulder. "We have to find that mole." I think of the RLWs again. I'm still not sure one of those silly princess wannabes is desperate enough to work with Alva, but it's the only lead I have. I can figure this out on my own.

"There's more." Jax looks gloomy. "Headmistress Flora was at Royal Manor this morning to meet with the royal court to discuss protection for FTRS. She's worried about Alva's manifesto and what it could do to the students at our school. The princesses were sympathetic, but..." Jax hesitates. "They refused to offer protection. Everything that has happened at FTRS makes us too risky to help. We're on our own."

"How could the princesses say that?" I ask angrily. "We're kids and members of this kingdom. They're just going to let our school keep getting attacked?"

Jax's smile is grim. "You sound like Flora. Rapunzel said she stormed out right before the other princesses took leave and the gargoyles attacked."

"That's just like royals to think about themselves," I grumble.

Jax throws his hands up. "You are so anti-royal."

"I am not anti-royal!" I say. "I'm friends with you, aren't I?"

"You did refuse Princess Rose's invite to join the RLWs," Maxine chimes in.

"Seriously?" Kayla's jaw drops. "That's the most prestigious group in school."

"If they'd let boys in, I'd totally join," Ollie adds, pulling three balls out of his pocket so he can juggle. "Looks like a great way to impress the ladies."

"I have no desire to be a wannabe royal." I sniff. "I don't need their approval. All I care about is finding this mole."

"Gilly's right," Kayla agrees. "We have to find out who is secretly aiding Alva. She won't stop 'til she's ruling Enchantasia, and she wants the students of FTRS to help her get there." Her face scrunches up. "I have an idea, but you might not like it. There's only one person out there who can help us find that mole fast." She inhales. "Rumpelstiltskin."

Ollie misses one of the balls he's juggling and all three fly out of his hands, bouncing off the floor, the walls, and Maxine's head.

"No price is worth paying for his help," Jax reminds her.

I glance at Kayla. After what Rumpelstiltskin did to her family, I try to avoid saying his name at all costs. Say it three times, and rumor has it, he'll appear. We don't need any more problems. "There has to be another way to find out who the mole is." We're all quiet.

"What about my mini magical scroll?" Maxine exclaims. "Someone is leaving me messages on it. It has to be someone who works at *HEAS*."

Jax and I look at each other. "She has gotten several notes. We should check it out," says Jax.

I sigh. I'm still not convinced those messages are for Maxine, but what other lead do we have?

"I can prove my messages are real! What if we showed up at *HEAS*'s offices in the village?" Maxine asks. "If they see me outside, they might be willing to talk."

"Sure," Ollie says. "We can just pop out of the castle and go to *HEAS*. Maybe we can even pick up fresh flowers and caramel cakes while we're there."

Jax scratches his chin. "I think Maxine is onto something." She beams.

"Did you eat too much gingerbread?" Kayla laughs. "Last time you tried to break out, you set off every alarm in the castle and had Wolfington on you in seconds. You can't bust out of a reform school."

"You used to disappear all the time," I remind her.

"But I never left school grounds," Kayla says, giving us a glimpse into a world I've wondered about. "Gottie—excuse me, Alva—would leave me notes near the Hollow Woods. I've never broke out. It's like asking for a longer sentence in this joint."

A sly smile spreads across Jax's face. "So maybe we don't break out. We *walk* out."

Pegasus Postal Service

Flying Letters Since The Troll War!

FROM: Anna Cobbler (2 Boot Way)

TO: Gillian Cobbler (Fairy Tale Reform School*)

*Letter checked for suspicious content

POST RETURNED TO SENDER. RECIPIENT REFUSED DELIVERY. AGAIN.

CHAPTER 6

Delinquents on a Roll

I wake up to the glow of our magical chalkboard scroll lighting up our room like fireflies. I squint to read the lettering that appears and know immediately the time has come to make our move.

All classes canceled today due to plumbing problems in the cafeteria. A buffet will be set up in the gymnasium today for all meals. Take time to study and enjoy the lovely weather!

—Headmistress Flora, FTRS

I throw back Kayla's pink covers to wake her. She stops snoring and blinks at me. "Flora canceled class. That's our sign! Ollie is probably already at the meeting point. Go! Go! Go!"

Five minutes later, I'm wearing the clothes I arrived at FTRS in and Kayla is unhappy about wearing some of my other peasant threads. We move quietly through three moving hallways without being spotted, but Kayla keeps stopping to braid her hair. ("My hair should look good if my outfit doesn't!")

"Come on!" I huff as a new hallway opens up a few feet away. How this girl used to sneak around to meet Alva, I'll never know. "Before we're—"

"Oh, hello, Gillian Cobbler!"

Kayla and I spin around. Princess Rose is even more beautiful up close. She looks fresh as a rose at 7:00 a.m. in a lilac gown and a tiara. Her blond hair is pulled up in a bun that has a matching bow, and her satin skirt swishes as she walks toward us and shakes my hand with a delicate touch. "It's so lovely to finally meet you." I notice the RLW packet in her hands. "Where are you off to so early and dressed so…humbly?"

"I told you our clothes looked sad," Kayla whispers in my ear.

"We're headed to the gym to exercise. Like my father always said, 'A day started late is a day wasted.'"

The princess beams. "I couldn't agree more. That's why I'm up early too. The Royal Ladies-in-Waiting are hosting a tea for a visiting princess from the kingdom of Captiva this afternoon. I do hope you'll be joining us."

So that's what that fluffy pink thing was in our dorm mailbox. "I'm really busy."

Princess Rose steps closer and smiles. "Yes. Exercising. Strange how you will manage to do that when the gym is being used for food service today."

Fiddlesticks. I've been made. Not a great way to start a breakout. "I guess we'll get some fresh air then. Maybe hike."

Princess Rose holds my stare. "Hopefully you'll be back in time for tea. Tessa tells me you have not accepted our invitation. May I ask why?" I start to fumble under her ice-blue stare. "You were the one student I asked for by name when I was given this position."

The way she's staring at me makes me feel like I've fallen into poison ivy. "Thanks, but I don't think I'm royal material." I look down at my muddy boots.

Princess Rose puts a hand on my arm. "The

Royal-Ladies-in-Waiting can teach you all you need to think like a princess. Don't you want to feel and act royally? Have the chance to leave the FTRS grounds and visit Royal Manor?"

I burst out laughing. "Sorry," I say when I see her shocked reaction. "Thanks for the offer, but being royal has never been something I've aspired to."

The sleeping beauty raises a perfectly arched eyebrow. "That's a shame. Being royal is the quickest way to gain power in Enchantasia, and power is something we *all* need more of. Like your father. It would be a shame if his new-found power as glass-slipper maker disappeared again." She pushes her glossy hair away from her eyes. "From what I've heard, the extra income that comes from being related to you has helped your family tremendously."

I feel a pit form in my stomach. Is the princess blackmailing me into joining?

Rose hands me a pink card that smells like roses. "If you change your mind, here is a new invite. I hope you'll reconsider." I start to take the card and feel a tug. Princess Rose won't let go. Her smile is thin, making her lips look like pulled taffy. "I won't be happy 'til you're a member, Gillian."

"Yes, Princess." I grab the card and pull Kayla to a new

hall that appears. I don't even curtsy. See? I'd make a terrible RLW, but I am tempted by the thought of leaving school grounds and not getting detention for it.

"She didn't ask me to join the club," Kayla grumbles as we hurry away.

"You helped Alva try to curse the royals. I don't think you're being invited."

Kayla sighs. "You have a point."

We pass the elf cleaning crew dusting an atrium sitting area where books are tucked into bookcases as high as the stained glass windows. Some of the feather dusters are dusting on their own. The elves seem to be on a coffee break because they don't move when they see us hurry past. Minutes later, we're at the cafeteria.

"Over here!" Ollie whispers. He, Maxine, and Jax are hiding behind a sign announcing fencing tryouts with Blackbeard. *Ye Better Be Prepared!* it says. Same goes for today. My friends are in disguise wearing Gnome-olia Bakery uniforms and chefs' hats. The sight of Jax in a baker's apron makes me giggle.

"What?" He models his apron. "I'd make an excellent baker. Put yours on. Our ride leaves in five minutes."

I throw mine on and take in the heavenly scent of cinnamon. "What's the plan?"

"Gnome-olia Bakery is doing its weekly delivery of cinnamon rolls." Ollie points to the kitchen. "We will sneak in the back of the carriage and make like a bag of rolls. They should have extra sacks that we can slip into. These uniforms will help us blend in at Gnome-olia Bakery 'til we can make our way out."

Maxine gives me a toothy grin. "Gilly! You came! The *Happily Ever After Scrolls* office is next to the fountain in the village square. We'll need to find a way to sneak in there once we can scout out the location. I even posted a message on the *HEAS* comments board by my last note and said, 'Would love to visit the office!' And look what someone commented below me: 'It's right next to my favorite tea shop. I'll have to wear my new Little Red Riding Hood cloak there if I'm ever invited.' It's got to be our source!"

"Wow." I think Maxine is right. This source wants to help us!

"We're going to find the mole! We're going to find the mole!" Kayla sings.

"I agree, but I still have one question," I say. "Gnome-olia delivers here every few days. How are we getting back?" Their faces fall.

Ollie swallows hard. "We're clever. I'm sure we'll come up with something."

"Just two more sacks, Gemma!" someone yells, and we duck down to avoid being seen by the school's goblin chef.

Jax motions for us to follow him. I hate coming into a heist without all the information, but the thought of seeing Anna washes my concerns away. I stuff the baker's hat on my head and follow the others through the cafeteria. One by one, we drop to the floor and crawl along behind the counters. The wood countertops are filled with strange, half-chopped root vegetables, and pots are steaming on the cast-iron stove. Some are being stirred by long, wooden spoons bewitched with magic. Jax pulls me behind a sack of potatoes.

I see boots under the table. "Don, Headmistress Flora wants an order of caramel cakes. We're having a tea honoring Princess Rose. She just joined the staff."

"You've got a royal working in a reform school?" asks Don as we move around the table to the other side to avoid them. Maxine is moving so fast that she narrowly misses hitting a wayward pot with her big feet. "I think I have some in the carriage. Hey, Phil!" he calls. "Grab me a dozen caramel cakes for the headmistress."

I hear more footsteps. "I'll sign the scroll for the delivery then and be off," Don says.

Our group scurries behind a sack of flour that is the size of a giant. If Phil comes down our aisle, we're toast.

"Where is that scroll?" Gemma asks. "I had it on the counter." I see the purple nails of her goblin feet inch closer to where we're hidden. Then she turns back. "It's gone! Oh well. Come into the cafeteria and I'll grab a new one."

Ollie holds up the missing scroll. "Let's move." With the coast clear, we crawl quickly along the pan racks and we're out the door in seconds. Into the cool, misty morning air we hurry, standing up and diving into the back of the carriage. I grab the first sack I see and begin passing them out. Ollie and Kayla fit into one. Maxine has her own, and that leaves one for Jax and me. I hear voices and know we only have seconds to hide.

Jax jumps in and shakes the bag for me to join him. "Let's go, thief!"

I'm out of time. I grab his hand and hoist myself into the burlap sack rimmed with flour and crumbs from rolls. Jax pulls the sack over us. Through the fibers of the bag, I can just make out Jax's face staring back at my own. I hear one of the guys approach the carriage and tie down the back of the canopy, shrouding the area in darkness. We're off.

CHAPTER 7

Breaking Free

An hour later, I can barely believe my eyes. I'm home. We've ditched our bakers' clothes, slipped out of Gnome-olia Bakery without pinching cinnamon rolls, and are now standing in the middle of Enchantasia village square. The fountain still gurgles and sputters like a geyser every hour on the hour. Peddlers bustle by with their carts, selling trinkets, mini magical scrolls, and Rapunzel's hair-care products. Villagers bang into us on their way to work or school while Pegasi fly overhead, dropping Pegasus Posts to homes, boots, oversized teapots, and other shops.

I hear the clock tower chime 9:00 a.m. and scan the crowd for my siblings. They should be on their way to trade school, and I know they used to pass right through the square so Felix could make a wish at the fountain. Just beyond it, I spot the gold-colored building with the famous quill-and-scroll sign—*Happily Ever After Scrolls: Enchanting Enchantasia with the News One Scroll at a Time!* There is only one main door, and goblins, trolls, and pixies are flying through it on their way to work. How are we going to get past them? How are we... Do I smell shoe polish?

Home. Father's shop is just around the corner. I haven't seen our crowded boot in so long, but with it just feet away, I feel a longing. I begin to walk toward the square that leads to our street and feel my arm yanked back.

"Don't be foolish." Jax holds my arm. He and Maxine are leaning against a wall near the farmers market. "The square is way too public. We need to keep our heads down and stay out of large areas."

"But—" I protest.

Jax's violet eyes are all knowing. "I can tell what you're thinking, thief, but it's too risky. You can't visit your sister."

My heart sinks.

Maxine pulls her scroll out of her pocket and glances at it again. "I'm so nervous! What if my mystery note-giver didn't see my post on the *HEAS* comments? What if she forgets to wear a red cloak? What if we can't get inside? What if…?"

I place a hand over her mouth. "What if we wait and see what happens?"

Ollie walks over holding a shabby cloak. "New disguise for Gilly! Look what I nabbed! These babies were waiting by Goodwill." He offers me the cloak.

"Why do I need a new disguise?" I ask.

"You're famous! I've seen people staring at you," Jax explains. "People know you're at FTRS. If you're recognized, we'll be toast. Put these on and try to stay in the shadows. You can be our point person."

What? That's just…gingerbread! When did my hero work suddenly become a liability? I tie a brown cape that smells like molasses around my shoulders. I tuck my brown hair in and pull the hood over my head, tying it tight so it doesn't fall off. "If I'm the point person, I'll alert you if I see Pete and his goons. I can spot the Dwarf Police Squad from three carriages away."

"Mmm, do you smell that?" Ollie asks, closing his eyes and inhaling sharply. "Caramel cakes. I haven't had one since I was on the high seas."

The clock in the square chimes nine fifteen. "Okay, here's how it's going to go down." Jax sounds in command. "Maxine and I will scout out the security at the building, making Maxine's presence known. Maybe her source will see her and come down. Everyone look for a person in a red cloak. If that doesn't work, we'll try to get inside. Gilly, you're on point for the Dwarf Police Squad. Kayla, you look for alternate exits along with Ollie, who will pretend to be a shopper in the square. If anyone spots us, we meet at the Pegasi valet stand. Got it?"

"Huh?" Ollie's eyes are watering, and his tongue is sticking out of his mouth. "They're oozing caramel and—whoa! They dunked a patty cake in caramel! Caramel inside and outside the cake. Genius! Would it be so wrong if I pinched one?"

"Ollie," we moan.

"They won't see me swipe it!" he insists. "If I juggle apples and do the ear trick, they'll be so distracted that they won't even notice."

"No patty cakes." I turn him away from the cart and toward a vendor selling satin gloves. "Look like Ella!" the sparkly, glowing sign screams. "If we get caught, we're doomed. And we still don't know how we're getting home yet."

"We'll worry about that after." Jax uses a calming voice I associate with royal speeches. "First, we need Maxine's source to show herself and talk. We have to find that leak in the castle before—"

Maxine burps. "Sorry! I'm nervous!"

"Oooh! Look at those Ella gloves!" Kayla coos.

"Patty cakes!" Ollie stretches his arms out to the sweet cart.

This is why I usually work alone. Our crew is a mess. I can do so much more without all these distractions. "Everyone," I say sharply. "We broke out of FTRS. We could be spotted at any moment. Flora might figure out we're missing. Let's keep our eye on the dragon."

Jax nods encouragingly. "Exactly! Places, people."

But I guess I had no reason to worry. There is a reason all of us are in FTRS. We're good at pretending to be what we're not. Once everyone is focused, our plan falls into place. Jax takes Maxine's arm and the two begin walking over to the *HEAS* offices, talking animatedly about a puppet show they supposedly just saw.

A few seconds later, Kayla skips along behind them, never getting too close, never stepping too far away. "Look!" I hear her cry to no one in particular. "Six pence! Anyone want to help me throw some in the *HEAS* fountain?"

Ollie pulls his cloak tight as he peruses the peddler carts. "If I could just find some gingerroot flowers or stems, I'd get an A on this class project," he says loudly.

Too bad gingerroot is harder to come by than fairy godmothers. Maxine found some once (ogres have an excellent sense of smell), but I used it on Jocelyn when Harlow escaped. Maxine and I should really hunt near the Hollow Woods for some more.

I lean against the brick wall of the Pied Piper's Music Emporium where I can see the whole square laid out in front of me. There's no sign of Pete or Olaf. In the distance, the silver turrets of Royal Manor blind anyone who dares look at them too long. I focus on the cobblestone path around the fountain that leads toward 2 Boot Way. I'm so close and yet so far.

I see Jax and Maxine inch closer to the *HEAS* doors. I can see them whispering and pointing to a shining silver box on the front of the door. Is that a security system to get inside? A speaker? I hate not knowing what is happening! I could help break into that joint. I know it. The flurry of workers going into the building has stopped. The foot traffic in the village square has thinned out, and any hope I had of bumping into Anna or my siblings is growing slim. The only children out now are too little for schooling. I notice Kayla hand a small child a coin for the fountain.

My eyes linger on a boy carrying a blue balloon with his mother. He bops the thing up and down, reminding me of my little brothers Han and Hamish. Another tug and the balloon flies away. His mother makes an attempt to reach it, but the balloon is now almost at the top of the clock tower. The kid is wailing when, just as suddenly, the balloon begins to descend.

I watch as a woman shrouded under a red velvet cloak reaches for the balloon and catches it in her hand. It's the source! She's come! I want to scream it out and tell the others, but that will blow my cover. I wait patiently for Jax and Maxine to turn around or Ollie to look my way so I can alert someone to what's happening. They're all in their own little worlds. I watch as the woman in red hands the balloon to the squealing child and the mother, who stares in disbelief.

"How the heck did she do that?" I ask myself out loud.

The woman in red looks my way as if she can hear me. I

feel my fingers tingle. Her hood hides her face in darkness, but I can see just the corners of her mouth turn up in a smile that I seem to recognize. The question is from where? It's not Alva. Returning a balloon wouldn't be her style.

"Thief!"

I turn and see a woman at the caramel cake cart pointing to Ollie, who is holding a bag of patty cakes. "Thief!" One hangs from Ollie's mouth. He quickly drops a smoke bomb. "Stop him!"

"Ollie," I groan. When I look back for the woman in the cape, she's gone.

People screech as the smoke bomb's cloud of gray smoke grows. Villagers start running in every direction. Ollie takes off toward the Pegasi valet stand just as the sound of hooves gallop into the square. I don't see Maxine or Jax. Strangely, Kayla is sitting by the fountain like she doesn't have a care in the world.

"What seems to be the problem?" I hear Pete the police chief ask from atop a horse that makes him look taller than his three-foot height. Olaf, his half-ogre sidekick, walks up beside him, making the ground shake. I crouch behind a barrel of water that a horse is tied to.

"It was a boy! About this high, just stole a whole bag of my cakes and then set off a smoke bomb to get away," the peddler explains. "I think he went that way."

"Looks like another FTRS candidate, Olaf." Pete laughs. "Flora should give us commission. Which way, ma'am?"

"He went that way! Toward the Pegasi valet stand."

My hair stands up on my neck. That's our meeting point! If Pete finds Ollie there, he'll be caught. I need a distraction.

I stand up slowly even though Pete is just feet away, and I stare at the horse drinking from the barrel. "Hey, boy," I say, talking to the horse as if he can hear me like a Pegasi would. "Want to go for a little run?" I untie his rope and with a little push, the horse takes off at a gallop—right toward Pete, who pulls his own horse out of the way just in time. I use the ticking seconds of my diversion to go straight to Kayla, who is reading a small scroll.

"Kayla!" I shake her by the arm. "We have to go before Pete gets back."

"Those two! They were with that boy!" the woman says.

I turn around, and Pete and I make eye contact. I grab Kayla as Pete's voice rings out loud and clear. "*Gillian Cobbler!*"

Fiddlesticks. I've been made again.

CHAPTER 8

Fight or Flight

ᖰᖳ

Pete can't prove it's me if he can't catch me. I pull Kayla with me, bobbing and weaving through the carts as I hear Pete's horse grow closer. We need a distraction so we can get to the valet stand first and warn the others.

"Gilly, stop right there!" Pete gallops closer. That's when I spot the apple cart.

"I'm sorry," I say to the apple vendor as I pull his cart down on its side and apples roll into the cobblestone street.

"Aaah! Gilly!" I hear Pete screech as his horse stops short and Pete goes flying from the saddle. I watch him land on a bag of apples and wince. That had to hurt. "I'll find you!" he yells. "I always find you!"

I jump and weave over the apples, using Pete's momentary

downfall as a chance to duck down an alley that I'm sure leads to the valet stand. Kayla is slow for some reason, but I manage to slip into the Pegasi valet stand without Pete nabbing us. I blend into the crowd of royals and royal wannabes standing in a long line as Pegasi coaches pull up.

Doormen open approaching coach doors and usher in riders, and the next group takes off in flight as magic carpets stop by those still in line to drop off giant packages and heavy items. In their beautiful satin gowns and smart dress coats and with their arms filled with bags, these royals and wannabes look like they don't have a care in the world. I bet they don't.

"Psst, over here!" I hear someone say. I look at the back of the line and see Maxine, Ollie, and Jax crouched behind a pile of hay for the Pegasi. We rush over and I pull them to the water troughs where Pegasi are often not allowed to go and rest. I take one look at Ollie and punch him in the arm.

"I know," he sighs, his lips covered in caramel. "I had what Professor Harlow would call a relapse." He offers me a cake. "Want one?"

"We were this close to figuring out the code to the *HEAS* door," Jax says dejectedly. "We just needed one more person to go in so we could figure out the last number."

"Not that anyone noticed I was there!" Maxine says miserably. "Now we've busted out and are going to get caught for nothing," she adds.

"Not for nothing," Kayla says. "Look! A woman in a red cloak handed me a note." She holds out a small scroll. We grab it and read the scrawled wording.

STAY ON THE RIGHT SIDE. SCHOOL IS STILL THE SAFEST PLACE TO BE. AS YOU KNOW TOO WELL, KAYLA, DEALS CAN BE DANGEROUS. TELL YOUR HEADMISTRESS SHE WILL SOMEDAY REGRET MAKING ARRANGEMENTS WITH THOSE SHE DOES NOT TRUST COMPLETELY.

"She must be the person at *HEAS* who has been giving Maxine notes," Kayla says. "And now she is giving me one too. There must be a reason."

"I saw her in the square too, doing magic," I tell the others. "She seemed familiar. If she's really our source, she must know us somehow."

"Did you get a look at her?" Jax asks Kayla.

Kayla shakes her head. "I couldn't see her face. She moved

so fast, but I think she's talking about Rumpelstiltskin in this note."

Maxine covers her ears. "Don't say his name!"

"Do you think this source knows where my family is?" Kayla asks.

"I'm not sure, but she's definitely trying to help us, and she'll probably contact us again soon," Jax reasons, glancing around the crowded valet stand. "But if we want that to happen, first we need to get out of this village. My money is on taking one of these beauties." He nods to the Pegasi.

"Sure, let me just go into my dragon's tooth purse and take out my money for a ride," I say sarcastically. "No one is going to give us a lift, especially to FTRS. I say we go back to Gnome-olia and get a ride with them tomorrow."

"Ooh, the bak over soun grea idea." Ollie's words are muffled by a caramel cake he's stuffed in his mouth. I grab the bag and toss it. He looks like he might cry.

"No, we need to get back today," Jax insists. "Pete will alert the school otherwise. We need to hitch a ride with someone going our way. Like those two." Jax points to two girls who have just joined the back of the line. I'd recognize them anywhere by the curls in their hair, the long, green-and-royal-blue gowns, and the gloves on their hands. They're Flora's daughters, the wicked stepsisters, and despite whispers to the contrary, they are actually beautiful. And whiny.

I overhear Azalea. "You said we'd have time to go to Pinocchio's Puppet Theatre before we went back to school." She stomps her feet. "You never do what I want!"

Dahlia growls at her sister. "We're not even supposed to leave school grounds. We were supposed to get a few new gowns for the royal dinner at Royal Manor and then head back. We're supposed to be at Princess Rose's RLW meeting."

"Why would I want to help with her wannabe royal club?" Azalea pouts, her curls bobbing up and down as she shakes her head. "I want to *be* royal, not pretend to be."

"She asked for our help, and we're going to give it," Dahlia insists. "It's the quickest way into her inner circle. Mother said keep her close, remember?"

Jax and I look at each other.

"Now where is that magic carpet with our other packages?" Dahlia asks as the line moves forward. "If it doesn't get here with those shoes, this whole trip will have been a waste. Those glass slippers have been on special order for weeks!"

"Wait!" A girl in a simple tan-and-white apron and white dress scuffed with shoe polish is running. In her arms are four beautiful, shiny shoe boxes that are almost as big as she is. I see the stamp on the side and stare at it in surprise. *Cobbler Glass Slippers—Get the Original.* "Here you go, ladies!" she says. "The magic carpets were backed up so I delivered these freshly boxed shoes myself." The voice, the brown hair tied back in a bow, the new clothes and shoes... I know before she even turns around who she is.

"Anna." The name slips from my lips.

"That's your sister?" Maxine is in awe. "She looks just like you!"

"Is she a thief too?" Ollie asks, and I notice he got the cake bag back. Stinker.

I shake my head. "No, she's all sugar and sweetness."

"So you're opposites?" Jax jokes and I glare at him.

"Look at her boots!" Kayla marvels. "They're so glittery."

"Business must really be booming." I stare at Anna. "I can't believe saving FTRS helped boost sales."

"You didn't actually do it alone," Jax reminds me and I shrug.

We watch Anna try to hand Dahlia and Azalea the boxes.

"How are we supposed to carry those?" Azalea holds up her arms full of bags.

"We're out of bags," Anna says apologetically. "But I can wait with you 'til you get on your carriage so that you don't have to carry them."

"Obviously," Dahlia snaps. "That's your job."

Hearing them talk down to Anna makes my blood boil, but my sister takes it like a pro.

"Not a problem," she says sweetly. "Cobbler Shoes is happy to help."

"If she distracts Azalea and Dahlia, we can get in their carriage and hitch a ride back," Jax whispers. "We just need a diversion to get in."

"Anna won't even take my Pegasi Posts." I stare at my younger sister sadly. "She is not going to agree to help us."

"Attention, royals!" I hear Pete's voice and shrink back. "I am looking for a group of thieves who have hit the peddler square this morning." He rides down the line, and I cover my mouth to keep from laughing at the applesauce dripping down his shirt. Pete stops in front of Azalea, Dahlia, and Anna, who is trying to balance all the stepsisters' boxes. "Aren't you Gillian Cobbler's sister?"

"Yes," says Anna, sounding surprisingly stubborn like me, "but she's not here. *You* put her in Fairy Tale Reform School."

"Not today, sugarplum." Pete looks around the area with beady eyes. "She's broken out, and I'm going to find her and haul her back in. She'll be there 'til next year at this rate!" He laughs loudly and his horse jumps. As Anna moves out of the way of the hooves, one of the boxes in her arms topples off the pile to the ground. A glass slipper with a broken heel falls out.

"Look what you've done!" Azalea cries as Pete strolls on, talking to other passengers. "We waited weeks for those shoes!"

"I'm so sorry." Anna grabs the broken pieces and puts them back in the box. "I'll replace them." Her voice is shaky. "I can have a new pair ready next week."

"Next week?" Dahlia is irate. "You tell your father we need a new pair *today*."

"But"—Anna sounds nervous—"I don't know if we have any more. They're all special orders now and—"

"You have *one* hour!" Dahlia snaps. She looks at Azalea. "We can go to your silly puppet theater while we wait and then take the Pegasi from Cobbler's."

Azalea claps her hands. "Yay! We get to do what I want!"

Dahlia rolls her eyes and looks at Anna. "One hour. No more or we want our money back for *all* the pairs." She drops the rest of her bags at Anna's feet, and Azalea does the same. "You might as well carry all our bags while you're at it. You don't mind, do you?"

"No." Anna curtsies and I want to vomit.

Azalea and Dahlia waltz off. With no leads, Pete disappears too. That's when Anna bursts into tears, big tears rolling down her cheeks. I hear Maxine sniffle. She and Kayla knock me in the back at the same time. "Go!" they mouth.

I walk from my hiding spot and pick up one of the boxes. "Hi, Anna Banana."

She stops crying immediately. "I should have known. Go away." Anna tries to pick up all the boxes again and they tumble.

"Let me help. You know you can't manage alone, and you're pressed for time."

Anna holds a hand up. "I don't want to hear why you're running away from FTRS with your friends and leaving your family behind."

"Anna," I plead. "I'm not running away! I want to come home. That's why I'm here. I'm trying to find a way to stop Alva." My sister folds her arms and turns away.

"Anna?" Jax asks questioningly. I see the others slip out of the shadows. "I'm Jax. This is Kayla, Gilly's roommate, and our friends Maxine and Ollie."

Ollie bows. "Lovely to meet you, miss." He offers her the snack bag. "Caramel cake?"

"Gilly is telling you the truth," Jax says, giving Anna a magnetic smile. I can tell she's mesmerized already. "We're only in the village to gather information on Alva and the threat to the kingdom." He moves closer to my sister. "If we can stop her, Gilly will be able to come home. All she talks about is you and your siblings."

The corners of Anna's mouth turn upward. She catches me staring and frowns again.

"But if Gilly and the rest of us are caught, she'll be stuck at FTRS longer," Jax continues. "We have a ride back—Azalea and Dahlia—*if* we can get in their carriage. All we need you to do—"

"I'm not helping criminals!" Anna begins to walk away and Jax steps in front of her, putting a hand on her shoulder. He looks very royal standing there like that.

"We just need you to look the other way when we slip into the back of the carriage. That's it. In exchange, we'll help you carry all these bags back, and none of us will say a word about Gilly, your fight, or thieving. Deal?"

Anna is silent for a moment. "Okay."

Everyone grabs a package and we begin the walk in silence. It's just a few blocks, but we have to walk slowly to watch for Pete. We pass the Teakettle Twins' large porcelain teapot duplex, which has steam escaping from the spout, and Hansel and Gretel's candy-inspired cottage. I hear a lot of chatter near Mother Goose's Nursery Day Care, but we keep our heads down.

Soon, I see the familiar boot-shaped sign above Father's shop: *Cobbler Shoes*. Azalea and Dahlia's carriage is already waiting. Jax holds open the back of the carriage for us to slip inside. Maxine, Kayla, and Ollie go first. I begin piling in boxes and bags, and then it's my turn to disappear. I look at my sister standing there with her arms crossed.

"I love you, Anna Banana." She refuses to look at me. "I'll be home before you know it. I'm going to make you proud that I'm your sister."

Anna smiles ever so slightly. "You should get going. They'll be back soon."

I climb aboard and Jax gets in behind me. We bury

ourselves behind packages and go unseen when Anna adds a new, blue, glittered shoe box behind us a few minutes later. It isn't long before I hear Azalea and Dahlia bickering and climbing into the carriage in front of us. The Pegasi take flight and the packages around us shift, but I say not a word.

I just stare at my hands where the item I've had clenched in them has been hidden the whole time. The glass shines even in the darkness. I stare at the broken glass heel, trying to remember how poor our home and life were before FTRS, and how far my family has come since I became famous. I will never let it get that bad for them again.

Before I know it, the Pegasi are descending and we're back at Fairy Tale Reform School. We shrink back as the girls remove the carriage flap to grab their packages. They're so busy arguing that they don't even notice when one of them grabs my foot instead of the bag next to it. Finally, with the cart empty, they throw the flap back down and the carriage is quiet once more. Still, we wait. Jax and I look at each other, thinking the same thing. Within seconds, the carriage will start to move toward the stables. We'll get out there, and it will be as if we've never left.

I hear Maxine breathe a sigh of relief. "We did it!" she whispers a little too loudly.

WHOOSH!

A furry hand with long nails pulls the flap back, and I blink at the bright light of day. Professor Wolfington's hairy face comes into view, a devilish smile playing on his lips. Behind him, Headmistress Flora looks less amused.

"Ah, Miss Gillian, Mr. Jax, and company. Glad to have you back," Professor Wolfington says as if we've just rejoined the party. "We've been expecting you."

Happily Ever After Scrolls

Brought to you by FairyWeb—magically appearing on
scrolls throughout Enchantasia for the past ten years!

Students Break Out of Fairy Tale Reform School!

by Beatrice Beez

Five students at Fairy Tale Reform School sneaked off the grounds this morning in the back of a Gnome-olia Bakery carriage. Gillian Cobbler, beloved for her heroism in the battle to stop Alva, apparently led the charge that included Ollie Funklehouse, Maxine Hockler, Kayla Wingtip, and Jax Porter.

"I thought something smelled like stale bread when five young people wandered through the cinnamon roll department in oversized bakers' clothes," says Nigel Stuveson, senior cinnamon roll supervisor four. "Then we received a note asking us to look for a group of kids. I put sugar and spice together and realized it had to be that lot."

At the same time Nigel was calling the Dwarf Police Squad chief, FTRS also received a tip from an anonymous source about the breakout. By this point, the chief learned about the stolen caramel cakes and broken apple cart in the village firsthand. "I knew they wouldn't get far without help, so I checked the list of Pegasi flights in and out of FTRS yesterday afternoon and saw one leaving from Cobbler Shoes with the headmistress's daughters. I had a hunch they'd be in that carriage. Now we're looking into whether Gilly's sister was involved in helping her escape."

Further investigation found that Anna Cobbler, Gilly's younger sister, was an accomplice in the incident, and she has been given a first offense by the Dwarf Police Squad. (Three will land a child in Fairy Tale Reform School.) Headmistress Flora says her own daughters were unaware they had stowaways aboard their carriage and played no part in the students' disappearance.

Fairy Tale Reform School's chief critic, Millicent Gertrude, mother of student Ronald Gertrude, says this latest incident proves how important it is for visitation day to be earlier than planned. "I'm pleased Headmistress Flora has moved up visitation day," says Millicent, who tells *HEAS* that parents will visit the school in two weeks. "Parents need to see whether FTRS is a safe place for their children. With Alva and the Evil Queen on the loose, children cannot be escaping the school grounds."

While rumors of a Royal Manor break-in by gargoyles last week have not been confirmed or denied by the princesses, Headmistress Flora continues to stress that FTRS is the best place for wayward children to be in these dark times. "All the students involved have been reprimanded for their behavior, and school security procedures are being reevaluated. With students this clever on our roster, we need to stay vigilant."

Keep checking your Happily Ever After Scrolls *for more coverage on the search for Alva and Fairy Tale Reform School's woes!*

CHAPTER 9

Wicked Trouble

❧

"What were you thinking?"

I've never heard the Wicked Stepmother this unhinged. She's kicking up hay in the Pegasi stables as she paces in front of us, looking like she might pull every last hair out of her normally neatly wound bun. Kayla, Ollie, Jax, Maxine, and I are lined up like we're about to be sent to the gallows, while Professor Wolfington and Professor Blackbeard keep a watchful eye. Blackbeard's sword looks particularly menacing hanging from his scabbard. Madame Cleo is here too, having been beamed in by Miri's mirror in the stables, which has a horse motif etched in bronze on the frame.

"Stowing away in a Gnome-olia Bakery truck? Stealing a dozen caramel cakes? Evading the Dwarf Police Squad?

Breaking an apple cart? You broke out of Fairy Tale Reform School!" Flora repeats our offenses as if we don't remember them. "Do you know what havoc you caused for both the school and yourselves?" Her dark eyes flash. "Pete wanted to sentence the lot of you to another two years for this crime. You're lucky I talked him down to an additional three-month sentence!"

"Only three months?" Ollie sounds a wee bit gleeful. "That's awesome! I was thinking six at least."

"Me too," seconds Kayla, talking to Ollie as if they're the only two in the stables. "For a minute, I thought she was going to say a year. No one's ever broken out of school before!" The two high-five.

Flora unbuttons the brooch that clasps her tailored dress shirt closed and loosens her collar like this is all too much for her to handle. "And you two." She points a finger at Azalea and Dahlia, who are fidgeting uncomfortably and keep banging into the shopping bags at their feet. Flora begins looking through their purchases. "I took away your Magic Express cards, and yet somehow here you both are with bags from Combing the Sea, Pinocchio's Puppet Theatre, the Pied Piper's Music Emporium, *and* Red's Ready for Anything.

What's this?" She peers at the red lettering on the box as Macho and Mighty, Jax's and my favorite Pegasi, neigh a warning from their nearby stall. "Learn How to Defend Yourself Kits? Boxes of glass slippers and new gowns? Your shopping habits have gotten out of control!"

"But, Mother," Azalea whines, pulling at her pearls, "we're the only two girls at the Royal Academy without glass slippers! Everyone has a Cobbler pair but us."

A Cobbler pair? My name is famous! I'm starting to like this. Finally, our family has some respect.

"Too bad." Flora takes the boxes from the girls and hands them to Blackbeard. I watch Madame Cleo cast a spell through the mirror and *poof*! The boxes disappear. Dahlia whimpers. "They're mine for safekeeping," the Wicked Stepmother says. "I won't return them to the shop, because that would affect Gillian's father's sales, but you will not be receiving the shoes 'til you've learned your lesson about lying and spending."

"A walk on the plank would work," Blackbeard whispers in Flora's ear. I see her wince. Pirates don't have the best breath. "Have Cleo put a few sharks in the waters, and I promise those poppets will never touch a Magic Express card again."

Azalea begins rummaging in the one bag Cleo's charm missed. The Red's Ready for Anything Kit is still there, and Azalea opens it and pulls out something called a Quick Cover Stink Bomb that I can only guess she's about to toss his way.

"I can assure you, Miss Azalea, that the effects of that can in your hand are spotty at best," Professor Wolfington says, looking anything but alarmed. "May I suggest saving that for an unsuspecting garden gnome, perhaps?" Wolfington should know. He's tangled with Little Red Riding Hood before.

"Azalea, we do not spray teachers," Flora says wearily. "And that kit is going back." She turns to the pirate. "Thank you for the suggestion, Professor Blackbeard. I think I'll save the plank for another day."

"Aye. Suit yerself, lass." Blackbeard looks disappointed.

Azalea raises her hand. "We aren't reform school students." She glares at me. "So can we be excused? We were just in the village to go shopping."

Flora sighs. "Yes, but you should know that all of you students have two weeks of detention with Madame Cleo and Blackbeard." We groan. "And, girls, I will be by your quarters later to speak to you further." Azalea and Dahlia do a lot of huffing as they shuffle past us. I notice Azalea trying to hide a Pinocchio bag behind her hoop skirt, but Flora takes it out of her hands as she passes.

"How'd you even know we were missing?" I ask when they're gone. That is the part I still don't understand. It's not like we had to check in, since there was no classes. I smell a rat.

"I told them."

I turn my head toward the open stable doors and stare at the girl in black who has her arms folded across her chest. Jocelyn. (Professor Harlow always said a person's stance gives their mood away. That's one thing she was right about.)

"Why do you have to stick your nose where it doesn't belong?" I snap.

"Me?" Jocelyn looks like I just told her black was the new pink. "You're the one who Broke. Out. Of. The. School. I was doing you a favor! It's dangerous out there with Alva on the loose, and you sure as bread crumbs can't take care of yourself."

I give an exaggerated laugh. "As if you're worried about my safety."

"I'm not worried about you," Jocelyn snaps. "I'm worried you'll lead the rest of your crew into harm's way. You only worry about yourself."

I wish she would stop saying that! "Yes, wanting to see

your sister captured and Alva put out of commission to protect Enchantasia is very selfish," I say sarcastically.

"Thanks to you, your sister has her first FTRS offense."
Jocelyn holds up a mini magical scroll as proof and I pale.
They know Anna helped us? "Like I said, selfish. At least my
sister puts me first. She went off to spy on Alva and kept me
here where she knows I'll be safe."

Jax and I burst out laughing. "You think Harlow broke
out to spy on Alva?" I ask, looking at Flora, whose expres-
sion is blank. "You really are as crazy as your sister." Jocelyn
lunges for me, and Blackbeard extends his sword to keep us
both apart.

The Wicked Stepmother purses her lips. "Enough stalling!
Why did you sneak out of school today?" No one answers.
"Believe me, you do not want the amount of detention I will
give if you don't tell me what you were up to."

I refuse to say anything. It's just my way. Innocent until
you can prove me guilty! I look at the others, hoping they're
just as strong as I am.

But Kayla cracks. "We wanted to talk to someone at
Happily Ever After Scrolls because we think someone there
knows who the mole is in the castle," she blurts out.

The rest of us moan. "Kayla, remind me never to tell you my secrets," Ollie complains.

Kayla makes a face. "No! I've lied for too long. This time I'm coming clean. They can help us." She turns to Wolfington. "We're pretty sure someone there is sending Maxine clues."

"What clues, lass?" Blackbeard asks.

Kayla falters when she sees my face. "I...have this one we got today in the village. It mentions me." The teachers look at each other.

Wolfington takes Kayla's scroll and studies it. "Do you think it's been bewitched with dark magic?" he asks Flora.

"It doesn't appear to have any spells on it, but we can have Madame Cleo examine it closer." She puts it in her pocket and Maxine sighs. "You children know better than to try to tackle a problem like Alva on your own. Have you learned nothing from what happened last time?"

"Last time we saved the day," I remind Flora, who does not seem to like my answer. "We're onto something here."

"You children need to let us handle things," Professor Wolfington says. "We have eyes everywhere, and we'll take care of Alva and this mole."

"But—"

"No buts, buckaroo." Blackbeard cuts me off. "We got that Rumpel matey protecting the school and—"

"Professor Blackbeard!" Flora says.

The rest of us look at each other.

"You're letting Rumpelstiltskin protect the school?" Kayla asks quietly.

"That dude is crazy!" Ollie agrees.

"Did you ask him about my family?" Kayla asks. "Does he know where they are?"

Flora puts a hand kindly on Kayla's shoulder. "I'm sorry. He wouldn't talk about your family. He was here for reasons I cannot discuss at this time."

"Reasons that not all of the professors agree with," Professor Wolfington lets slip, and Flora's look is stern. "I believe there are better ways to protect FTRS."

"Agreed, darlings! We don't need his help here," Madame Cleo says.

"That is my choice and it's not something I want to discuss!" Flora is losing her patience. She glances at Blackbeard, who pretends to polish his sword. "But yes, he's protecting the school since the royal court would not. Alva is waging a war to take over this kingdom and using the students at our school to do it. I will not let all our good work be in vain, so yes, I made a deal with him and it's one I will have to live with!" She realizes she's shouting and stops.

"That's why you met with him?" Kayla's lower lip quivers. "You probably never even asked about my family! You don't care about me at all!" She runs from the stables.

"Kayla!" I yell. "Wait!" I turn to Flora. "How could you do that to her?"

"You can't talk to the headmistress like that," Jocelyn says.

"Since when do you stick up for the headmistress? Keep your nose out of our business!"

A loud wolf whistle silences our bickering.

"That will be quite enough," says Professor Wolfington. "You two must learn that in life we sometimes have to work with those we don't like to fight for the greater good." I open my mouth to protest and Jocelyn does the same. "I know you don't trust each other, but if we want to stop Alva, we're *all* going to have to work together. Understood?" We both nod, but I don't want to.

Flora runs a hand over her skirt to smooth it. "Now, please proceed back to your quarters and let us examine

Maxine's mini magical scroll. Saving the kingdom is not a job for children."

I exhale loudly and we all trudge out of the stables. Jocelyn is with us, much to my chagrin.

"Dude, we can't let Rumpel help our school," Ollie says. "He worked with Alva before, and he will again. Our professors have lost their minds! They'll never find the mole."

Neither will we at this rate. Our breakout was a bust! If we're going to find the mole, I need to get out of this castle and do some sleuthing on my own. But how do I break out again? There is no way out unless... The RLWs! They get to go to Royal Manor. Hmm... It couldn't hurt to get chummy with some of those annoying RLWs anyway. I'm sure one of them knows the mole the way they were going on about their mission to protect themselves. I'm onto something here! Hmm…I wonder what Princess Ella will give my family if I save the whole kingdom again.

"What are we going to do?" Maxine asks.

"I just remembered somewhere I have to be," I say as the others continue talking.

"We're kind of in a jam here," Jax says. "Don't you want to talk about this?"

"We can at dinner." I have no idea how long that royal tea is. "Or tomorrow!"

"Where are you going?" Maxine asks, but I don't answer. I run as fast as I can so that no one catches up with me.

I'm back in the castle and three hallways down when I finally see the gold plaque with a bouquet of fresh pink roses on the door. I don't bother knocking. I burst through the door. The RLWs see me and stop talking. Princess Rose steps forward.

"Um, is it too late for me to join in?" I ask, trying to sound proper and failing.

"Not at all. I'd be delighted if you joined us, Miss Gillian," Princess Rose says.

And just like that, I'm in—and ready to go undercover on my own.

CHAPTER 10

Simply Charming

◈

Princess Rose rings a bell, and the RLWs in attendance stop whispering and stand at attention.

"Thank you for joining me for today's special ceremony," she says in a reverent tone as I stand beside her and do my best not to cringe. "It's been two intense days of royal prep work with Miss Gillian Cobbler in my private chambers, but I am pleased to say today that she is officially ready to join you as a Royal Lady-in-Waiting!"

The RLWs clap demurely. They're dressed head to toe in pink (I'm still wearing my blue uniform) and have on pink sashes that look like Princess Rose's. She places one over my head, pins a gold rose pin on my lapel, and makes my welcome into the club official. The girls applaud louder. I think I'm going to throw up.

This is the first time I've been in the club chambers for more than a few moments. When I burst into their tea the other afternoon and announced my desire to join, Princess Rose explained that I would have to do some intense "royal thinking" with her before becoming a member. (I wasn't even allowed to stay long enough to have a tea biscuit.)

Turned out "royal thinking" was code for two days of lady training and questions like: "How would a royal slay a dragon?" Answer: "Have someone else do it for them." So far, Princess Rose hasn't said anything that has helped me in the mole hunt. If anything, spending so much time with her has only made my life thornier. I've missed meals with my friends and my excuses (Extra detention! Vegetable picking in the garden! Private fencing lesson! Magic Carpet extra help!) are wearing thin.

I just hope becoming a member of this club is worth my time. The smell of roses in this room is overpowering. So is the color pink on the walls, the carpet, and the cotton candy–tinted couches. I let my eyes adjust to the frilly lace curtains and throw pillows on every seat. Flora's daughters, Azalea and Dahlia, eye me skeptically as they stand there in rainbow-hued gowns. I have to watch what I say around those two.

"To Gillian!" Princess Rose cheers. She points a pink wand at the ceiling and confetti and balloons fall, nearly blinding me with glitter. Everyone cheers. A few pieces get in my mouth and I sputter. "Have a seat next to me," Rose adds, and sits in the center of her adoring group on a hot-pink throne. The princess is (shocker) wearing her signature color and her blond hair is pulled back in a long braid. I quickly tuck in my dress shirt, which I just noticed was hanging out of my skirt. This silly sash is making that easy task nearly impossible.

"Girls!" Raza, a sprite foreign exchange student from a reform school in Hadingford, jumps out of her seat in a very unladylike fashion. I'm just saying. "It's time for our pledge." The merriment in the room dies down as all the ladies stand, wave their handkerchiefs in the air, and face Rose. I try to copy them, but I haven't memorized the whole pledge yet. Tessa leads the RLWs as they speak in harmony.

"I solemnly swear that I will uphold the Royal
Ladies-in-Waiting pledge with my whole heart.
I will honor the royals who give tirelessly on
commoners' behalf by:

being a good and obedient servant,

answering our royals' call to duty whenever or
whatever it may be,

being the lady they need me to be despite my
common (or unremarkable) upbringing,

putting their needs before my own no matter
the cost,

and remembering that wearing this pink sash
means I am worthy of being a princess even
though it's impossible for me to actually be one.

Nevertheless, I will cherish the opportunity to
serve royalty to the best of my ability all the days
of my life and consider myself charmed."

Are these girls missing a screw or what? Worthy of being
a princess even though I can't be one? Charmed because I can
serve royalty?

Princess Rose gives them a standing ovation. "Charming!" She curtsies and they do the same. I tumble into Raza on my attempt.

"A few orders of business before we begin." Tessa produces a scroll. "The Royal Ladies-in-Waiting spent our day off this week shining glass slippers and jewels for the princesses under the watchful eyes of Pete and the Dwarf Police Squad, and we were so honored to do so! We are very much looking forward to visiting Princess Ivy's talk 'Sorcery: A Royal's Greatest Gift or Downfall?' and were pleased that our royal offering of lilies was accepted with charm by Princess Snow. Our next RLW fund-raiser—pink, scented handkerchiefs—is sure to be a huge seller at school," she adds with a squeak. "Who couldn't use a little color pick-me-up in our dreary school uniforms?" I bite my lip to keep from laughing.

"The royal court will be most pleased. Well, I know I will be," Rose adds somewhat sadly. "It pains me to know my fellow princesses have done nothing to help protect FTRS from Alva's wrath. My job is to serve you as you serve me, and I will stand by you and this school in its time of need."

"Thank you, Princess!" a girl calls out and everyone

curtsies again. The move happens so quickly that several girls and fairies bump heads.

"I know together we RLWs will prevail against evil," Princess Rose says. "Like Gillian here." She looks at me. "I've admired the way you've handled yourself at FTRS since the first day I saw you. Never becoming too much like the masses or conforming. Just doing what feels right."

I'm a bit surprised to hear this. "Really?"

"Yes!" She places a hand on my arm. "I myself am this way. Of course, you can only rest on one act of bravery for so long." She smiles thinly. "If you and your family are going to continue to be seen in a wonderful light, you have to think about what you will do to help Enchantasia next." My stomach plummets at the thought of my family losing what they've just gained.

She pats my hand. "Don't worry. You'll figure it out. You need to harness your own power. If you want something, you take it. Don't wait for anyone to give it to you," she says, sounding fierce. "That's what I'm teaching the girls. It's important to charm the world to get what you want out of it."

I've noticed the princess uses the word "charmed" a lot,

but the sentiment doesn't sound too shabby, if I'm being honest. Power is something I could use more of. Think of how I could use it to help my family and others! "You're a smart princess," I say and am surprised to hear the words come out of my mouth.

"Thank you!" Rose smiles. "My fellow princesses might disagree, but a princess in power can do so much more than just sit and look pretty in a carriage. Look at me. I'm making things happen that no one would expect from a former sleeping beauty. I don't just stay in the castle. I'm out at FTRS, meeting our people and working to help you all gain the power you deserve. Don't you deserve a say in how your kingdom is run?"

"Yes!" the girls agree, and I find myself saying the same. We all need a say in how things are done around here. The royal court is wrong to leave FTRS hanging, and Flora is crazy to not want our help when we offer it.

"Alva is offering power," pipes up a pixie in the back, and everyone turns and looks at her with a gasp. I listen closely. "She says if we follow her, we'll have a say in running the kingdom. All we have to do is join her side."

A troll girl speaks up. "Would that be so bad? If we're

with Alva, we'd have the kind of power you speak of, Princess Rose. No one messes with a villain." A few people mumble in agreement.

"Look at all the attacks on the Royal Manor and FTRS and in the village that have happened by being against Alva," Raza adds. "No one is able to stop her. Well, Gilly did for a half a second, but Alva will be back and this time she'll have numbers."

I can't believe what I'm hearing. I have to tell Jax and the others. I go to stand.

But wait. He doesn't know I'm here. I need to get more than pixie bread crumbs before I go blabbing about a discussion.

"Having power is something we all want more of," Rose says thoughtfully. "But you have to decide: Do you have power if you're following Alva's orders? I believe we should choose our own destiny. My goal is to make changes that will help everyone, not just one villain." We take in what Rose is saying. "We should start today's meeting. Azalea, could you tell us what's on today's schedule?"

Azalea stands and curtsies. Rose curtsies, the group curtsies, and I feel like we're going to curtsy back and forth for hours. Thankfully, Azalea produces a scroll and begins to read. "Today's Royal Lady-in-Waiting challenge is conversation starters. As we are working on our RLW conversation patch, we will practice having a chat with a fellow commoner and practice how to talk with a royal."

The consensus in the room is that this RLW patch is very exciting.

"To help with the project, Madame Cleo will be beaming in," Azalea adds as Dahlia goes to the magic mirror to dial up the Sea Siren who appears on-screen sporting pink hair and pearls laced into her sea-kelp top.

"Darlings! How wonderful to see you," she drawls. "I trust you're having a lovely meeting?"

"Yes, Madame Cleo," the girls say as if on cue. I forget to respond.

"Splendid!" She claps her hands. "As Princess Rose told you, today we will learn the dance of language." Madame is swimming back and forth across the screen. "As visitation day approaches, it is imperative that you show your parents how far you've come since you entered FTRS."

"Mastering a conversation shows your maturity," adds Princess Rose. "If you can go from talking to a royal to talking to a beggar, then you can appeal to the masses. Being adored has its rewards. People will follow you anywhere if they like what you have to say."

"So true!" says Raza with applause, but I'm rubbing my nose. All these roses in here are making it itchy.

"Let's start with a simple conversation about the weather," says Madame Cleo. "Miss Gillian, I'm so pleased to see you joined the Royal Ladies! And I love the new purple hair you're sporting! Why don't you and Miss Tessa start us off?"

Tessa and I face each other. She's wearing perfume that is competing with the rose scent in this room. My nose doesn't like it. Tessa extends her hand and I—

"*Achoo!*" I sneeze all over her face.

A dozen girls produce pink handkerchiefs at the same time.

"Oh my goodness, that will never do," tsks Madame Cleo. "You're supposed to cover your mouth when you sneeze and always turn away from your guest."

Great, I've failed already. "Sorry."

"Now, let's try that again," Rose encourages.

Tessa looks less than happy, but she musters a smile as she extends her hand. Darn curtsy. I make it halfway down, wobble, and come up, but I shake her hand.

"I'll go first," Tessa says testily. "Hello, Gillian. How is your afternoon going?"

Wow. Okay, so that's how it's done. "Fine. Thanks. How is yours?"

"No 'thanks.' Use 'thank you.' And use proper language, please," says Madame Cleo.

"I'm fine, thank you. How are you this afternoon?"

Tessa smiles. "Splendid, although this weather is dreadful, don't you think?"

"Yeah, it's as drafty in the castle as it is outside."

"No, no, no!" Madame Cleo covers her face with her hands. "Don't knock Fairy Tale Reform School. Why don't you take over, Azalea, and show how it's done?"

Azalea doesn't botch her curtsy. "We are pleased you could make the journey to our school in this nasty weather. Can I get you a hot beverage after such a long outing?"

Everyone applauds and Azalea accepts their praise with another curtsy. Then they all curtsy and I get dizzy. I can't take anymore. I need a break. Now. "May I be excused to get a glass of water?" I ask Rose.

I slip out of the room while the others watch Raza and another girl tackle "Complimenting One Another's Shoes."

Olivia follows me. "I could use a refreshment," she says. "We do so much talking."

"Yeah," I say, rushing out the door and taking big, gulping breaths to get rid of the rose scent that is overwhelming me. *Water. I need water.*

"The water fountain is down there," Olivia says, and I follow her down the hall, where elves are mopping the floors with mops that clean on their own. "I just love your purple hair. You have to tell me how you got it. It makes you look so powerful."

Powerful? "You think?" I touch my hair and Olivia nods.

"It would look even better if you wore it up sometimes so you can see the purple. Maybe in a side ponytail?" she suggests, and before I can protest, she pulls my hair to the side, removes one of her glittery bracelets, and uses it to fasten my hair. "Like this. Look!" She pulls me over to one of Miri's mirrors. "You look beautiful!"

"Beautiful? Me?" I ask, amazed at what I'm seeing in the mirror. My hair doesn't look half bad, and the glittery band makes it shine. I look almost royal. Olivia's pretty decent. I've never been given a present before. "Thanks," I say and then start to cough as I breathe in the rose perfume Olivia is wearing. It reminds me of the RLW room.

"Fiddlesticks, you need water," Olivia says. "Here! This way!" A gurgling water fountain is just beyond the elves' cleaning cart. "You take a sip first."

I hurry over and begin gulping sips in a very unlady-like fashion.

Olivia starts to laugh. "Gilly, stop! You are acting like an ogre! Look how sloppy you're being. Just like Maxine!" I stop drinking and look up in surprise. "Oops! Sorry. I forgot you're friends with ogres, and your roommate is a fairy who almost destroyed FTRS." Olivia looks almost embarrassed for me. "Some of the girls thought you weren't RLW material because you were friends with them. Not me, of course, but people do talk about the company you keep."

My face burns. The RLWs are talking about me? My stomach feels swishy and my cheeks burn. I'm used to people saying good things about me lately. I don't like the idea of them making fun of me. The words bubble out of my mouth like a volcano. "We're not friends," I blurt out. "Kayla was assigned as my roommate, and Maxine just hangs on everything I say and I can't shake her off." Olivia laughs.

"I would never be friends with an ogre like her." Olivia laughs harder, and I feel some satisfaction in changing her mind. "I mean, have you seen the way she drools over every…" Olivia suddenly stops laughing. I notice the mops stop mopping. The elves pull their cleaning cart to a new hallway. Olivia starts to move away. I feel the hair on the back of my neck stand up and I turn around.

Maxine and Jocelyn are standing a few feet away from us, and it's obvious they heard everything I just said. Jocelyn looks positively furious, but Maxine is the one I care about. My heart is thumping loudly as watch the left side of her face droop. Maxine's right eye rolls wildly, and her left eye wells up with tears.

"You're so selfish, Cobbler! Maxine is your friend!" Jocelyn hisses. I'm too mortified to say anything. "I should have known you'd become an RLW behind our backs. You look like one with that ridiculous hairstyle, and you sound like one too."

"Maxine," I start to say.

"How could you?" Maxine asks, and starts to cry so loudly the window nearest me shakes. Then my former friend charges down the hall before I can stop her.

Happily Ever After Scrolls

Brought to you by FairyWeb—magically appearing on scrolls throughout Enchantasia for the past ten years!

Get Ready for Fairy Tale Reform School Visitation Day!

by CoCo Collette

Spurred by parent outcry, Fairy Tale Reform School has moved up its semiannual parent visitation to today. "I am pleased Headmistress Flora and the staff will finally let us inside this mysterious castle to check on our children," says Millicent Gertrude, mother of Ronald Gertrude, who has reportedly been begging for his early dismissal since Alva's manifesto showed up on school grounds.

Sources tell *HEAS* that FTRS parents are worried the magical scroll will spur students to join Alva's growing ranks. As *HEAS* reported earlier this week, Alva has joined forces with ogre tribes that were close to signing a peace treaty with the royal court. Rapunzel is said to be meeting with the ogres to try to sway their decision.

More of Alva's bewitched scrolls have also appeared

around the village, beckoning people to join her army. "Enchantasia will be mine," the scrolls declare. While the princesses say we have nothing to fear, the scrolls have made an already anxious Enchantasia increasingly worried about Alva taking over the kingdom.

Princess Rose is the only royal to make a statement. "In these trying times, it is more important than ever to celebrate wonderful events like FTRS's visitation day!"

According to spokesmirror Miri, parents are invited to attend a tea presented by the esteemed Royal Ladies-in-Waiting Club (run by Princess Rose), dine with their children in the cafeteria, and observe them in classes and activities such as synchronized snake-dancing and the after-school Magic Carpet Racing Club, as well as listen to a lecture from the school's newest professor, Blackbeard the Pirate. He'll be presenting "Why Being a Bit of a Scoundrel Can Prove Useful—Playing to Your Child's Strengths."

After last semester's disastrous Royal Day *and* Anniversary Ball, it's easy to see why there would be concern about security, but Miri the Magic Mirror cryptically says the school is under the strongest magical protection there is for visitation day. "No one is getting in this castle unless they're invited," she tells us. We at *HEAS* are not convinced, but one thing is certain: covering anything going on at Fairy Tale Reform School is an adventure!

Check your scrolls often throughout the day for updates on visitation day and the search for Alva!

CHAPTER 11

Royally Yours

W e need more pink, girls!" Tessa declares, frantically shoving baby's breath and carnations into a hot-pink pitcher atop a pink tablecloth covered with pink plates and teacups. We're in the observatory where the Royal Ladies-in-Waiting Club is hosting the visitation day tea this morning.

Or as I like to call it the Pink Threw Up in the Observatory Party.

"Are you sure?" Raza frowns at the pink balloons netted at the ceiling to drop down on visitors. Her eyes wander over to the pink banner that says *Royal Ladies-in-Waiting—We Are Honored to Serve Royalty!* and the pink roses that are practically suffocating the room. "Do you think we might have overdone it with our signature color?"

"Definitely not." I try to keep a straight face as I pretend to straighten the tablecloth—again—at Tessa's urging. ("I think I see a crease!") "You can never have enough pink, but ditch the carnations," I say. "You guys should know this from the RLW gardening patch you earned. Princess Rose is allergic to everything but roses."

I hear the bells chime and then the mirror in the room glows—of course—pink. "Attention, students!" Miri says. "Our visitors are entering the gates to FTRS. After they have gone through security with the Dwarf Police Squad, they will make their way to the grand foyer. Please meet your parties there and take them to your first assigned class or to the Royal Ladies-in-Waiting welcome tea *if* you've received an invitation."

The girls around me clap politely and curtsy to one other. All the curtsying this week has given me a lot of lower body strength. Who knew curtsies were a workout?

"And now a message from Headmistress Flora," Miri announces.

"Students, we hope you have a wonderful, productive day with your visitors. You have all made such progress, and I'm thrilled your parents will get to see that firsthand. Have fun, be on your best behavior, and remember," Flora adds, her voice stern, "if you see something out of the ordinary, say something to one of your professors immediately."

"We're all in this together," we repeat as we have been saying and writing on banners around school. Alva's manifestos have been popping up all over Enchantasia, calling more citizens to join her army. No one seems to know how to contact the fiendish fairy to join, and yet somehow her ranks are growing. Jax has been sick over news that the ogre tribes wouldn't listen to Rapunzel and signed on to work with Alva instead.

I only know this from a terse Kayla. I've been so busy with the RLWs that I've barely seen my friends in days, which might be better. Maxine bursts into tears every time she sees me. But what can I do? I tried bringing up Maxine's name twice to Tessa and Raza, and they changed the topic to napkin-folding ideas.

"*Psst.*" I look to see where the noise is coming from, but the RLWs are all arranging flowers. I go back to smoothing my tablecloth. "*Psst.*" I hear again.

"Did you say something?" I ask Veronica, a sprite creating a goblet tower in the shape of a glass slipper.

"No," she says, sniffing. "I'm too busy working, like you should be."

Whatever. I go back to tablecloth smoothing, even though there is nothing left to smooth, but I keep hearing "*psst*" so I stop and try to see where the noise is coming from.

"Up here!" someone whispers. I look up and see Jax sitting on the ledge of a stained glass window near the rafters. He gives a little wave. He must have climbed into the room from outside. This boy loves to climb things.

"No boys allowed," I hiss, hoping no one notices me talking to the ceiling.

"This is the only way I could talk to you," he whispers back, his legs dangling close to Raza's head. "You're with these royal wannabes twenty-four seven."

"We are not royal wannabes," I huff. "A RLW's purpose is to help the princesses function to the best of their abilities, set an example for the villagers around us, and find inspiration from the royal court's royalness to harness our own power!" I gasp. "Holy gingerbread. Did I really just say that?" I sit down in a pink velvet chair near the window and breathe in and out. Jax jumps down from the ledge, and several of the girls scream.

"Boy! With the RLWs!" Tessa points at him like he's a villain. "*No* boys allowed!"

Jax straightens his dress shirt and gives her a perfect bow, bending all the way to his waist. "My ladies, my most sincere apologies for the interruption. You're all doing splendid work transforming this simple space into a tea worthy for a king, and I do not want to take away from that. I only ask that you allow me a moment to speak with this young lady here, who is my dear friend, and then I will depart."

Whoa. Jax sounds just like a prince charming!

Tessa's jaw drops. Olivia holds a handkerchief to her mouth and begins to giggle uncontrollably. "Um, okay, yeah," Tessa stammers. "I mean yes, sir! Take a moment."

"And may I suggest you hang the royal crest higher than the Enchantasia flag?" Jax adds. "In Royal Manor, the court's flag always flies above the kingdom's."

"I can't believe we forgot that." Tessa nudges Raza, who rushes over to fix the banners hanging on one wall. "Thank you." Tessa curtsies. Olivia curtsies. The rest of the girls curtsy. I do the same and fall into Jax, who catches me.

"It's all in the balance," Jax explains. "As you bend from the knees, pretend you're about to sit back in a chair."

"Forget the curtsy," I say through gritted teeth.

"You clean up nicely, thief." Jax touches my pink sash and the pink ribbon wrapped around my uniform waist. I self-consciously touch my head. My hair is pulled into another side ponytail courtesy of Olivia who has given me a pink flower for my hair. "You could definitely pass for a royal."

My cheeks burn. "I could *never* be a royal." I fiddle with the rose pin I got at my ceremony. "I'm just playing a part to get information." Olivia walks by with a box of dishes and I frown. "Olivia, those are the bread plates, not the tea biscuit ones. You need the plates with the small gold rim for scones." Her goblin ears flutter before she rushes back out of the room to the RLW storage closet to get the right plates.

Jax clears his throat. "Yes, I can see you're doing a great job *pretending*."

I pull him behind a giant standing floral arrangement. "Princess Rose is always talking about power being in the hands of the people, not the royal court. It's sort of empower-ing, you know? Why should the princesses get to decide what happens in the village? They don't live there. We know better what rules need to be made for ourselves."

Jax raises his right eyebrow. "How much pink fruit punch

have you had at these meetings? Like Wolfington always says, kingdoms need a leader to guide them and that's what the princesses in the royal court do. They've faced evil and know how to fight it. Alva won't give the people power. All she cares about is her vendetta."

"If the royal court cared about us, they'd protect FTRS, but they're not," I point out. "At least Alva is offering people protection!" I clap a hand over my mouth and sit down again. "Maybe I have drunk too much pink fruit punch."

"It's the rose scent in here." Jax wrinkles his nose. "It's overpowering. Let's get you outside for some fresh air."

I shake my head. "Princess Rose will be here any moment. I can't leave."

Jax sighs. "We need your help. The mole has gotten to the ogres. What's Alva going to find out next? If someone keeps feeding her information, she's going to learn FTRS is protected by Rumpel and then she'll try to squash that deal too. We're running out of time."

"That's why I'm here," I say. "To find out who the mole is. They're always talking about the manifesto in this club. Someone has to know the mole." I glance at Olivia. "Olivia! Rose wants pink swan napkins, not knots!"

Jax doesn't look convinced. "Is that why you didn't tell us what you were up to?" I'm quiet. "I miss my partner in crime." I blush. "Doing dirty work is not the same without your help, thief. Why'd you keep this club a secret?"

"I...I don't know why I didn't tell you," I say, and Jax stares me down. "Fine! I didn't tell you because I thought I could find the mole on my own, okay?" He makes a face. "But now that I'm here, it's not as awful as I thought it would be." I feel my face grow hot. I can't believe I just sort of said I like the RLWs. I *have* drunk too much pink punch!

Jax is quiet. "This doesn't sound like the thief I know. Neither does the conversation Jocelyn says she and Maxine overheard between you and Olivia."

My face burns. I can't believe Jax knows what I said. I'm mortified but also angry. Now my friends—some former, I guess—are talking about me behind my back? "Princess Rose requested me specifically," I say heatedly. "I can't help it if I'm the only new pick they made this term. Princess Rose thinks I have real leader potential. Who knows what I can accomplish if I follow her lead? If she likes Father's work as much as she says she does, maybe she'll let Cobbler Shoes even expand to new kingdoms," I say wistfully. "My family could have vacation boots to live in! For so long I've been judged for doing the wrong thing. Can I help it if I like the attention that comes from doing something right?"

Jax puts a hand on my shoulder and I notice the other girls watching us. "Thief, Princess Rose only helps herself. Rapunzel told Father that Rose hasn't been at one princess meeting this week about the ogres. She claims she's too busy here, and yet we all see her in *HEAS* scrolls getting her hair done at Rapunzel's Coiffures and having tea with Little Bo Peep. I don't know what's going on with her lately, but watch yourself. Your true friends would never turn their backs on you." He pauses. "And the old you would never turn your back on them either."

"Good morning, ladies!" Princess Rose waltzes into the room in a bright-pink gown and a giant tiara. She spots me with Jax and falters. "I see we have a visitor."

Jax bows again. "Princess, it's an honor to be in your presence." The RLWs erupt into giggles that can't be hidden behind handkerchiefs. "Excuse the interruption. I was looking for Miss Gillian."

The princess actually blushes. "Such manners! Ladies,

this is a young man who knows how to be an RLW, not that we have any young men in the club."

"Why is that, Your Highness?" Jax asks, and I can tell he's up to no good. "A young man can be just as accommodating to a princess as a young maiden. Maybe even more so. We could be of use when strength is needed, like now when you are carrying such a large box." He walks over and takes it from her.

"I've never considered a male RLW, but you make a valid point," Rose says as he places the box on a table. "Thank you for bringing the matter to my attention, Mr...?"

"Mr. Jax Porter." He bows again and a few girls sigh.

"You look sort of familiar," Rose says, looking at him curiously.

"My father is a farmer in the kingdom, Your Highness, but we have never had the pleasure of visiting Royal Manor. I hear it is quite lovely. Have you been back recently? I know you've had many meetings up there this week."

Stinker.

"No, I've been quite busy, but I must get back soon," Rose says, quickly changing the subject. "Ladies? Please gather round before you escort your families here. I have presents!" Princess Rose opens the box and takes out a stack of electric-pink sashes. The words *Royal Ladies-in-Waiting* are written in glittery, silver calligraphy that actually glows. "They're rose scented. A wondrous touch if I do say so myself. And they're enchanted," says Princess Rose. More applause all around. We all get in line to take one. "Make sure the bottom of the sash hangs to your left, just like we princesses wear them when visiting the kingdom."

Jax clears his throat. "I apologize, Your Highness, but don't you mean to the right? That's how I've seen it when you've graced us with your presence in the village."

She frowns. "Silly me! You're right, Mr. Jax. How perceptive of you." She peers at him again. "Are you sure we haven't met before?"

"No, sadly, and I'm afraid my father is working today and cannot visit so I will be with my friends Ollie's and Maxine's families."

"Aren't they ogres?" Olivia shivers. "I thought the ogres work with Alva now."

"Not all ogres," Jax corrects her, and I can't help thinking about the fact that their families are meeting and no one invited me. They must know what I said about Maxine. My stomach churns and I try to push away that funny feeling I'm having.

"Well, I bid you farewell. Ladies." Jax bows to the room again and slips out.

Raza sighs. "I do hope we'll see him again."

"Perhaps we will have to invite Mr. Jax and some other gentleman to a future tea," says Princess Rose. "As for today's, I have some disappointing news. I am disheartened to say that Princess Ella and the rest of the royal court declined my invitation to join us." The girls collectively gasp, and Princess Rose wipes away a single tear. Her face becomes defiant.

"Rapunzel says they find it too risky to visit FTRS during these trying times, but I disagree. Now is when we must show a united front. There is power in numbers, as I keep telling you. Sometimes I wonder if Alva could be right in wanting to change how Enchantasia is run." Surprisingly, some of the girls around me nod, and I try to remember their faces. I could follow them later to see where they go and if they talk to anyone suspicious. "But I fear I'm crazy to think such things."

The bells chime, signaling the end of this period. "That

is all. Please bring your families back so I may greet them. And remember your curtsies!"

I step into the hallway, hoping to see Jax and explain my behavior, but the hallways are too crowded for me to find anyone. Fairies are hitching rides on the backs of trolls, and goblins are walking hand in hand with gnomes. Everyone is smiling like Madame Cleo taught us in the Charming the World: Learning How to Put Your Best Magical Self Forward seminar we had yesterday. My new sash is glowing so brightly that students keep turning around to stare.

"Help! I've been blinded by a sash! Help!" Ollie walks toward me, and I smile with relief. At least he's still talking to me. He's dressed like a pirate complete with a skull and cross-bones belt. He covers his eyes. "I can't have a conversation with you when I can't even see you."

I jab at the sash to turn it off, but it's no use. "Just look straight ahead and I'll talk." Ronald Gertrude waves to me as he rushes by. I don't wave back. "You're not mad at me?"

"I don't *want* to be mad at you," Ollie says easily as we head to the FTRS foyer where we can hear the band playing. I see the FTRS cheer squad performing with magical pom-poms and some of the Magic Carpet Racing Club zooming around the foyer and sprinkling confetti, which the elves try desperately to clean up just as fast. Our teachers are greeting families as they enter through the large wooden doors. "What happened with Maxine doesn't sound like the Gilly I know."

There's that weird feeling in my stomach again. "I…"

Ollie cuts me off. "Oh look! There are my parents!"

His parents are tinier than I expected. Ollie brings them over and I notice his mom smells like biscuits. She has on a simple dress that reminds me of something Mother would wear. I remember Ollie telling me his parents are bakers who provide meals to docking ships at the Enchantasia seaport.

"Mother, this is Gilly Cobbler," Ollie says, making introductions.

She smiles warmly and clasps my hand. "Ollie has told us what a help you were during the attacks here. I'm glad he had you to help him rescue the royals."

Um, have they read their *HEAS* scrolls?

"I couldn't have saved FTRS without her," Ollie says without looking at me.

"So where is this Professor Blackbeard you wrote about?" Ollie's father asks. "You say he knows the pirate whose ship you were a stowaway on. If so, I'd like to have some words with him."

"Father, he carries a sword," Ollie reminds him. "At. All. Times. Oh look! That must be Maxine's family! Wow, her dad is so huge that his head hits the ceiling!"

I jump slightly at the towering sight of Maxine's family, especially after what I said about Maxine. They make Maxine look like a mini ogre. I have to remind myself that ogres don't eat people. That's a big, fat, ol' myth. Are there bad ogres out there who stomp on villages? Sure. But there are also bad humans who train gargoyles to destroy schools. Maxine sees me standing with Ollie, and I smile tentatively. She looks away as Jax walks over and shakes hands with Ollie's parents.

"You must be Gillian! You're just as Maxine described you," Maxine's mom says, and I try not to stare at her sharp teeth or the warts on her chin. "Maxine has written us about your friendship."

I think I might throw up. Maxine's such a good friend that she didn't even tell them what I said about her. "I care about Maxine a lot," I say awkwardly.

"Mother, these are my good friends Ollie and Jax,"

Maxine says to her parents and everyone shakes hands. "We'll find my friends Kayla and Jocelyn later."

Wait. *Jocelyn?* What?

"Look at your sash," Maxine's mom gushes, drool spilling from her mouth. "You're a Royal Lady-in-Waiting? Maxine has wanted to be one forever." I'm so embarrassed I wish I could reach up, grab a magic carpet, and disappear.

"Mother, we should really get to our tea," Maxine says. "I'm sure Gilly has to get her parents and escort them to the *exclusive* RLW tea."

"FTRS has been the best thing to ever happen to Maxine," her father interrupts, scratching the horn on his head. I wonder if Maxine will eventually grow one. She's pretty cute in comparison to her parents, who she once told me are one hundred fifty-two and one hundred fifty-three years old. "So much safer here than out there with all those manifestos popping up in the villages."

"We had one show up in the seaport the other day," Ollie's father says, looking way, way up at Maxine's dad. "I wouldn't let myself read it. What if it's magically bewitched to make a person follow Alva's orders?"

"That's what I think happened to all our ogre friends in

Tailsmen," says Maxine's mom sadly. "And we were so close to signing a peace treaty for all ogres too."

We grow quiet at talk about the ogres teaming up with Alva. As if I wasn't depressed already about how awkward things are between me and Maxine or how distant I've felt from my friends the last few days. And that's when I hear it. A faint voice that makes me feel like I'm home.

"Excuse me," I say politely. I walk swiftly toward the sound of my name.

"Gilly! Gilly!" Trixie yells. "Father, I see her!" She rushes toward me with Felix on her tail. They hug me so hard that I almost fall backward.

I look up just in time to see Father and Mother walking toward me too. I feel like my heart might explode. Anna is with them.

CHAPTER 12

Be Careful What You Wish For

I want to run to my parents and throw my arms around them, but Princess Rose says a lady never runs. (Exception: if they are in mortal danger.)

"Mother, Father, Anna," I say demurely and curtsy. Everyone looks at me. Trixie and Felix burst out laughing. Father clears his throat and my siblings stop.

"What a lady you've become." Mother hugs me. "Madame Cleo was just telling us about the etiquette class you're in. It sounds like you'll be practically royal when you leave Fairy Tale Reform School."

"Gilly?" Felix sputters with laughter. Even Anna shoots him a nasty look, but I can't stop staring at them. They're in beautiful new clothes that look like they were made by a tailor rather than on Mother's old sewing machine. They all have proper haircuts, and Father is wearing a spiffy hat that looks like a Mad Hatter original. Business really must be good!

"Why don't we head to the Royal Ladies-in-Waiting tea?" I look at Anna hopefully. "Princess Rose is looking forward to meeting you all."

"Can we see the wicked fairy scroll?" Felix asks, and families around us gasp. "I hear there's one in the castle too. I've never seen one."

"And you should never look for one," I insist, holding him by his shoulders. "Stay away from those manifestos. The one in the castle is closed off."

"That's exactly what I said," Father tells me, and we share a rare smile.

Trixie takes my hand, and Mother puts an arm around me as Felix talks a mile a minute about what has been going on at home. Cobbler glass slipper sales are through the roof. Han and Hamish are at Mother Goose Pre-K today. ("It's the golden egg party, and they really want to win," Trixie says.) I expected Anna to be silent, but Father is equally so. We shared a moment last time he was here, and yet today he looks worried and is wiping his forehead with a handkerchief.

"I can't believe you're a Royal Lady-in-Waiting," Trixie coos. "Can you, Anna?" She nudges my sister, then touches my glowing sash. "You've wanted to be one forever!"

"Yes, well, thanks to Gilly, I'm one step closer since her tricks in the village got me a warning." Anna gives me a nasty look.

I forgot they knew about my breakout. Father must be furious with me. "I'm so sorry about that. You see—"

"Anna is old enough to take care of herself," Mother says stiffly. "If she wants to be foolish enough to aid you and your friends when you're sneaking out of school, then she must pay the consequences. We already know you have two weeks of detention. Headmistress Flora sent a Pegasus Post."

"Yes," I say, failing to mention how Princess Rose sweet-talked Madame Cleo into letting me serve my time with extra RLW sessions. "It's been very trying."

"*Trying?* Curtsies?" Anna asks. "Who are you kidding?" She storms off, but I see the hallway in front of her waffling.

"Wait!" I put an arm out to stop her, and the hallway seals up in front of her. Anna is stunned.

"That. Is. So. Cool!" Trixie squeals when a new hallway opens in its place.

"The hallways are magical," I explain. "You need a map to get around this place."

"Do you get a wand?" Trixie says eagerly.

"Now, Trixie, you know you can't have one of those 'til you're twenty-one and have taken Wand 101," Father reminds her.

"We have training wands," I say, hoping this will impress Anna. She's always wanted her own wand. "We were allowed to take them out for a test run a few weeks ago. They have a number of spells programmed in them but they only worked for an hour."

"Is that why you now have some purple hair and a weird hairdo?" Felix asks.

"No, my hair was cursed, but it's fine," I say quickly when Mother raises an eyebrow. Anna glances at me, intrigued, then looks away. "My friend did my hair today and I like it."

Felix frowns. "It's not very you."

We're almost at the RLW tea when a new hallway takes us in a different direction and I get completely turned around. I've been so overwhelmed with all my new RLW duties and this fight with my friends that it takes me a minute to get my bearings. When we find a new hallway, I practically throw my family through the opening. We land in front of the observatory where light music is playing and Raza and Tessa are at the door handing out roses to guests on their way in. The way Mother gasps at the gift when she's handed one makes me feel guilty. I can only imagine how Maxine's mom would have reacted. Trixie and Felix race in after Mother, but Father hesitates.

"Anna, your sister is waiting to take us inside," I hear him tell my sister.

My sister folds her arms across her chest stubbornly, looking a lot like...well, the old me. "I'm not going. Not until you tell her about the note you received this morning."

"Anna!" Father scolds, sounding a lot like...well, how he sounded when he used to yell at me. "I told you we are not bothering your sister about this."

"Why not?" Anna demands. "It's her fault we're even getting scrolls!"

"Show me," I insist to Father, feeling nervous. "I want to know what's going on."

Father sighs and pulls out a piece of parchment. The

handwriting in this note is different from the one Kayla received, and the message is menacing.

> YOU have riches and a famous daughter,
> but I can take it all away. If you care about
> your family, tell Gillian to be a charming
> girl and do what she's told.

I feel ill. My biggest fear is there on paper taunting me. I peer closer at the parchment, noticing an extremely long, golden hair. A clue! I pluck it and place it in my pocket.

"I found the note tucked into our morning scroll," Father tells me quietly. "Your mother doesn't know. A clipping of the story on your breakout was with it." He gives me a look.

I ignore that part. "Why didn't you call the Dwarf Police Squad? They can protect our boot!"

Father shakes his head. "We're obviously being watched." He pats my hand. "I don't want you to worry about this."

"What? If Gilly just stays out of things, they'll leave us alone," Anna rants. She looks at me. "Let someone else fight Alva."

"But I'm getting closer. I can feel it," I protest. "I can do this on my own. Imagine the reward the royal court will give us then. Princess Rose really likes me! If I could find the mole in the castle, they might be so amazed by me that they'll give us a bigger boot or land or—"

"Do you hear yourself?" Anna throws her hands up. "Since when do you care about a bigger boot or more money? You sound just like the wicked stepsisters!" I gasp. "Can't you be happy with what you already have? Family and friends who like you? This note obviously means you're supposed to do your time here quietly and get out." I try to talk over her. "Oh, I forgot! You never listen, do you? You always have to be the *hero*."

My stomach is sloshing so much that I can barely stand. I feel suddenly very ill. "Anna!" I go to grab her hand, but she pulls away and storms off.

"Anna's right," Father says quietly. "This is a fight you can't win alone, Gillian."

"But I work just fine alone," I protest. "Why do I need help? Sometimes you have to do your own thing so others don't get hurt."

"Working alone is how you *do* get hurt," he reminds me. "You beat Alva last time because you had a team. Sometimes being a hero means being brave. Other times it means knowing when you need help."

"You're right," I say, and Father looks as surprised as I feel that we're agreeing. I think of what Jocelyn said. I have been selfish, and I haven't been a very good friend. I can't screw things up for my family, but I can't let the kingdom just fall apart either. I feel completely stuck. For a moment, all I want is to be small and on my father's shoulders. "I'm sorry. I guess I haven't been thinking straight," I admit. "But if me being part of all this hurts your business, I couldn't bear it. Everyone looks happier than I've seen them in ages."

Father looks at me. "I don't want you to worry about my business. We'll be fine whether I make glass slippers or not." I bite my lip. "You do whatever you have to do to help end this reign of terror with Alva *with* the help of others. Then we'll all be home together. Deal?"

"Deal." I'm not sure how I'm going to pull this off though. "I should find Anna before she gets lost." I hear the sound of a piano and frown. I think I'm missing the Royal Ladies-in-Waiting pledge. Tessa will be furious. I was supposed to chime the triangle.

Father nods to the door. "You go find Anna. I can distract

them while you're gone. I'll say you had a sash emergency."
He chuckles to himself.

I give Father a peck on the cheek—another unusual thing
for me—and dash down the hall. Anna could be anywhere.
Rumor had it they were going to shut the magical hallways
for visitation day, but they haven't. I tiptoe past the lecture
hall where I can hear Blackbeard speaking ("Like the sea, lads
and lasses have mighty tempers! Dealing with them takes a
plank—or a plan…").

A sudden left sends me past the choir room where students are singing "The Gingerbread Man" to a rapt crowd.
On the other side of the hall, I can hear Madame Cleo leading
a group of parents and students in the Fire Step. Miri appears
in a mirror a few yards away to scold two fairies who've
flown out of Wolfington's reading of *Enchantasia through the
Magical Years*.

I duck into a hallway to my right to avoid being seen and
come face to face with the entrance to the vegetable garden.
There's no way Anna's out here. I try to turn around and trip
over a watermelon, landing on my face and smashing the
watermelon with my fall. The melon juice drips down my
arm and my chin. I hear someone roar with laughter.

"Well, if it isn't the newest RLW!" Jocelyn say in a self-satisfied voice. She's sitting on a picnic blanket with Kayla, who grimaces at the sight of me. "Shouldn't you be more graceful, Cobbler? Oh, I forgot. You skipped that part of your training and went straight to being a backstabbing royal wannabe and a lousy friend."

I cannot stand this witch. I pull on Jocelyn's skirt and take her down with me. She lands in watermelon juice. Then I take a piece of watermelon and chuck it at her.

"Stop it, Gilly!" Kayla says, rushing over and helping Jocelyn up. Not me! "Just leave us alone and go back to the RLWs and your family. They're who you want to be with anyway."

"Leave *us* alone?" I question. "You would rather hang out with Jocelyn than me?"

"Yes." Kayla holds her head up defiantly.

"*Ha!*" Jocelyn says.

"She may be rough around the edges, but at least she's honest," Kayla continues. "She doesn't pretend to be someone she's not—like you. How could you hurt Maxine like that? She's your friend—we all were—and instead of sticking up for her, you cut her down to win favor with Olivia and the RLWs."

"Kayla! Jocelyn!" Maxine comes bounding into the vegetable garden, crushing several melons in the process. "Come meet my family and—oh." Maxine sees me, and the left side of her face falls. "I'll come back later."

I feel like I've been socked with a bag of flour. "Maxine, I…"

"Maxine, *stay*," Kayla insists, and Jocelyn giggles with wicked glee. "We're giving Gilly a piece of our minds. She needs to know how she's made us feel." She turns to me. "You haven't been around at all since the breakout. It's just RLWs, RLWs, RLWs!"

"Yeah," seconds Jocelyn. "For someone so anti-royal, you sure seem to have made the glass slipper fit, so to speak."

I've had it with Jocelyn chiming in. "If you must know, I joined the RLWs because I thought someone in there might be the mole or know who the mole is!" I glance at Maxine whose face is hanging to the floor. "I never wanted to take the sash away from Maxine. I joined because Princess Rose wanted me and I knew if I could get close to the group, I could find out information. The RLWs are obsessed with power."

Jocelyn raises an eyebrow, her dark eyes narrowing. "Sound familiar?"

"If it was all a ruse, why didn't you make them ask Maxine to be an RLW too?" Kayla questions. "Because you didn't want to be made fun of. You knew they were being mean to her, and you let them do it."

"I don't want to talk about this," Maxine says miserably.

"Admit it!" Jocelyn cries. "You like being the hero and getting the glory all to yourself! That's why you went it alone and left your friends flat like stale gingerbread!"

"This is not your business!" I shout so loudly that even Maxine quakes. "This is between me, my friend, and my roommate!"

"Roommate?" Kayla questions. "Some roommate you've been. I know I lied a lot to you when you came here, but I was doing it for my family. All you've done lately is think about yourself! You never stopped to wonder what your friends were doing or how I'd feel about it being visitation day and having no visitors," she adds. "At least the others invited me to be with their families today. You're my roommate, and you didn't even ask if I wanted to meet your parents or how I was feeling."

"Exactly!" Jocelyn says, twirling her cape with glee. "You guys have wanted to stop Alva since the beginning, but it's obvious Cobbler no longer remembers the prize. What have you found out by being an RLW, huh? I doubt anything. Meanwhile, Maxine has gotten another message on her scroll, and you don't even know what it is because you're too busy practicing curtsies."

"I…" My heart is beating fast. And there is that feeling in my stomach I had the other day. I can hear Jax in my head and Father and even my own thoughts telling me what I already know: Jocelyn and Kayla are absolutely right.

"I considered you guys my family at FTRS, but I was wrong about you," Kayla says. "I could never be family with someone so selfish."

I sit down on the bench and steal a piece of the crumb cake they have on their picnic blanket. They probably lifted it from the cafeteria this morning. "You guys are right about everything."

Jocelyn holds out her ear. "Can you repeat that?"

"I said you're right," I say gloomily. I glance at Maxine. "I was so worried about fitting in with the RLWs that I said some rotten things about Maxine, who has been kinder to me than anyone I know."

"I haven't been kind?" Kayla sniffs.

"You both have been," I continue. "I didn't mean what I

said—any of it. I was foolish and rotten, and I hope you can forgive me and let me make it up to you." I remove my RLW sash and place it over Maxine's head. It gets stuck around her neck. "This is for you. If they don't let you become an RLW, then I won't be one anymore either."

I glance at Kayla. "I got carried away. I should have thought about how visitation day would make you feel. Of course, I want you to meet my family. I want both of you to meet them!" Jocelyn coughs, but I ignore her. "Can you guys forgive me?"

Maxine starts to blubber and Kayla sniffles. "Yes, we forgive you!" Maxine cries, and she and Kayla hug me.

"Don't ever act like a wicked stepsister again!" Kayla says, and we all laugh.

Jocelyn gives a lackluster round of applause, and I turn on her. "What are you still doing here?"

"Be nice," Kayla tells me and my jaw drops. "Jocelyn has been helping us while you were off being royal." I feel my cheeks burn. "She's been hanging near the manifesto to see if anyone tries to contact Alva, and she's been doing what she can to track down her sister and convince her not to turn evil again."

Sisters. "I have to find Anna," I remember. "She's run off."

"I'd run away if you were my sister too," Jocelyn mumbles.

"I have to go back to Mother and Father," Maxine tells us. "Come join us at lunch when you've found Anna." We hug again and Maxine trudges off.

"Why did Anna disappear?" Kayla asks.

"We had an argument," I say quietly. "It sounded a lot like the one we just had. I wish I could wave a wand and make this week go away." *Wands*. If I were a girl who wanted one, the wand room would be the first place I'd go. "I think I know where she is."

"Well, don't leave us here." Kayla pushes the empty crumb cake box under the bench. "Maybe we can help talk to her."

"I'm in too." Jocelyn smirks. "I want to watch you get yelled at again."

I give her a look, but I don't want to get on Kayla's bad side again. "Fine."

The three of us step inside the castle and find the hallways shifting fast. I wonder if their magic is malfunctioning. "I'll never find the wand room with the halls acting like this."

Jocelyn removes a small pouch from her skirt pocket.

She pours purple sand into her hand, mumbles words I can't understand, and then blows the sand into the air. Within seconds, the sand is stretching out kernel by kernel down the hall, making a left near a giant sea-serpent water fountain. "This way," she says triumphantly.

I follow behind her, wondering how Jocelyn's magic slips under Miri's radar. *Because she's learned it from Harlow*, I realize. The former professor always had a free pass in her own school. We reach the wand room and find it locked.

"We should have known they wouldn't let students have wands today," Kayla says. "Where to next?"

I frown. "I don't know. If you were visiting FTRS, where would you go?"

"The Pegasi stables," says Jocelyn, blowing more sand into the air. But Anna is not there. The fencing demonstration has cleared out too, and there is still no sign of her.

"Maybe she left," Kayla says.

I shake my head as a family with a map walks by us talking about the Arabian Nights' Flying Carpet Tutorial. I wanted Felix to see that. "You have to be signed out."

"Well, we can't keep roaming the halls!" Jocelyn's voice makes a pixie family walking by the fireplace we're standing in front of jump. "Miri is going to catch up with us eventually and I, for one, don't want any more time in detention for helping you."

"I was fine finding my sister on my own," I snipe.

"Um, guys?" says Kayla.

"Yeah, it looked like it," Jocelyn retorts.

"You're the one who asked to come along!"

"Guys! Look!" Kayla shouts over our bickering.

The fireplace has rotated to reveal a hallway behind it.

CHAPTER 13

Past the Point of No Return

The hallway smells like it hasn't been opened in years. I cringe at the sight of all the moss and water dripping down the bricks, but I can't help but be curious. Flora built this castle. There must be a reason there is a secret door here. A door that's starting to close. Jocelyn and I both jump into the unknown, having the same reaction to pull Kayla through with us. Then the door closes and we're enveloped in darkness. Jocelyn quickly produces an orb of light. Her dark eyes peer back at me.

"Thanks a lot. Now we're stuck here!"

"You went through first!"

"Only because I knew you were going to if I didn't."

"Guys?" Kayla grips my arm. I can hear her wings fluttering. "Someone's talking."

We grow quiet to listen. I strain to hear anything other than dripping water and what I think is a squeaky mouse. Then I hear faint voices speaking quickly.

Jocelyn's and my eyes find each other, and I know we're thinking the same thing.

Alva.

Kayla begins backing away, her wings fluttering at warp speed, but I grab her, realizing something.

"It's okay. Alva wouldn't want to stay hidden," I say.

"But Rumpelstiltskin might," Jocelyn tosses out, and we both look at her. "So would that mole you're desperate to find."

The three of us say nothing, but we move onward. As the path begins to turn down and brighten, Jocelyn is forced to extinguish her orb. The voices grow closer, and I can finally make out what they're saying. *Gillian.* Kayla grabs my arm.

"Gillian can't know what is going on," I hear a familiar voice say and stop. *Flora.*

"Use her as bait," comes a second voice eagerly. "Gillian is the one she wants. If you hand her over to Alva, she might leave FTRS out of this hostile kingdom takeover."

I feel like I might spin into the ground.

"Don't you think I know that?" Flora sounds angry. "I've tried everything I can think of to avoid it. You know Rumpelstiltskin. His deal protects the school grounds, but not, it turns out, the students. That little troll. He knew that meant Alva's manifesto could still persuade students to join her cause. Wolfington has been leaving the grounds every night for weeks to try to see if there is another way to stop Alva, but we have nothing. Those children keep mucking up any progress we make with their snooping."

"You had to have seen that coming," the other voice replies. "None of them hold a candle to my sister."

Harlow! An outlawed villainous former professor and the headmistress of our school who is supposed to protect us are meeting up! I should have known.

Kayla and I look at Jocelyn, whose breath is coming so hard that I worry she might collapse before I do. She lunges forward, and Kayla and I grab her. Gosh, she's strong. I lock my arms around her shoulders and try to drag her to the ground with me. The ground sounds so good right now.

Harlow wants Flora to give me over to Alva to save the FTRS students.

What does that mean for me?

For my family?

"A sister who is beginning to ask questions!" Flora continues. "If she knew…"

"She mustn't," Harlow says. "Flora, you gave me your word."

"I know, but now you want me to use Gillian as bait and—"

"Your word," Harlow presses. "Leave Jocelyn out of it while you can. I have enough trouble. I don't have much time. I'm meeting with Rapunzel this evening."

"How's that going?" Flora asks.

Harlow sighs. "You know princesses! I must go before…"

"Yes, I know." Flora sounds frustrated as we hear the familiar whizzing of Harlow whisking herself away in a puff of smoke that slowly billows toward us.

And then I realize. If Harlow is gone, then Flora will be leaving too—and there's probably only one way out of here. "Up," I hiss. "She'll be coming back any second."

We run out of the passageway and down the hall so fast that I don't see the person in our path. *Smack!* Our crash sends the person flying backward where she lands on her butt. And that's when I notice the pink dress, the tiara on the ground, the crinoline of her skirt over her head. Fiddlesticks. We hit Princess Rose.

"Princess!" Kayla cries, hurrying to help her up. "Are you all right?"

"Yes." She adjusts her skirt. I don't have the heart to tell her how messy her hair is. She looks at me stormily. "You were supposed to be at the RLW tea an hour ago!"

Um…

"Dress emergency," Jocelyn says quickly and points to my skirt. "Gilly knew you said to wear pink today, and she had gotten some glue on her gown so we were trying to help her magically get it off. Obviously we didn't have much luck."

Wow, that was smooth.

"Gilly!" I hear my sister calling my name. She's smiling and running toward me, which is odd. "I've been looking for you!"

"I guess I haven't been alone," Princess Rose mumbles.

"I got a little lost and wound up sitting in on Professor Wolfington's history of Enchantasia lecture, and then I got to see a magic carpet tutorial." Anna is wound up like a top. "It was amazing! Then I visited the Pegasi stables. You're soooo lucky to go here!"

"You don't *want* to go here," I correct her, but Anna gasps at the sight of Rose.

"Your Highness, how wonderful to meet you." Anna's curtsy is far better than any I've managed. "I'm sorry we're late to your tea."

"Ladies." We turn to find Headmistress Flora staring at us darkly. "Whatever are you doing in this part of the castle? You are nowhere near the Royal Ladies' tea."

Our headmistress was meeting with Harlow. Anything she says is a lie.

"I was looking for Gilly," Rose answers for us. "Her tracker lead me here."

Wait. What?

"Tracker?" Flora looks dumbfounded.

"Her new sash," Princess Rose says as if it should be obvious. "It has a tracker in it." Flora's eyes nearly bulge out of her head. "These sashes are one-of-a-kind priceless beauties. I couldn't risk visitors—or our own criminally prone students—stealing them."

"But I took mine off and gave it to Maxine," I say.

Rose points to the rose pin I'm wearing on my lapel. "But you're still wearing your pinning ceremony pin. That's a tracker too. I know where you all are at all times!" she says happily like this is a good thing.

I'm flabbergasted. Flora seems equally so. "You tracked the students?"

"Yes," Rose says, growing impatient. "Now I really need to get back to our tea! A hostess should never be gone for too long. Neither should the cohost when she's invited a new student to join the club without asking." She looks pointedly at me.

Maxine.

When I open my mouth to speak, a siren blares through the castle.

"What's happening?" Anna covers her ears.

"We're under attack," I say, grabbing her hand, "but don't worry, we'll be okay." Rumpelstiltskin is protecting the castle. For the moment, that comforts me.

A mirror nearby glows green. "Headmistress Flora," Miri says urgently.

"What's happened?" Flora asks. "There can't be a break-in. We're protected!"

"They haven't broken into the school, Headmistress," Miri says, and it's the first time I've ever heard the normally steady mirror sound shaky. "It's Enchantasia…" The words seem stuck to her mouth like glue. "The ogres, the gargoyles… Alva. They've…burned half the village to the ground."

Happily Ever After Scrolls

Brought to you by FairyWeb—magically appearing on scrolls throughout Enchantasia for the past ten years!

Breaking News: Enchantasia Village in Ruins

by Beatrice Beez

The Enchantasia Dwarf Police Squad is ordering all residents who still have their homes, teakettles, and boots to stay indoors while the police investigate the village for ogres and gargoyles on the run after today's devastating attack. This reporter has toured the village with police protection and has noted that three blocks of boots, several teakettles, and storefronts including Mother Goose's Nursery School—as well as the famed Three Little Pigs' homes—were destroyed in the attacks.

Thankfully, the quick thinking of Jack and Jill, who were headed up the hill to fetch a pail of water, alerted the village to the incoming ogres, and villagers were able to get everyone to safety. In the village square a new magical scroll with an ominous message was found: "A regime change is coming. Join me or perish. The royal court can't save you."

Following the attacks, dozens of villagers fled the scene to join Alva's army. Rumor has it that students at FTRS have gone missing as well. "No one knows how they're contacting Alva, but we suspect there is a traitor in our midst who is helping them do so," says Pete, the Dwarf Police Squad Chief.

Rapunzel was visiting the village right before the attacks occurred, but thankfully left early for a hair-care ad luncheon. Meanwhile, the royal court is said to be scrambling to make a statement about the attacks, but they've already been beaten to the punch by one of their own. Despite imminent danger, Princess Rose signed her Royal Ladies-in-Waiting Club out of Fairy Tale Reform School to distribute fresh water, blankets, and food to magical creatures in need. Headmistress Flora was rumored to be against this idea, but as she is under questioning about her school's magical protection that left it untouched, she was unable to stop the princess.

"While my fellow princesses figure out the right words to comfort a village, my Royal Ladies and I choose to get on the ground and help those in need," said Princess Rose when we caught up with her at the Mulberry Bush shelter where she was giving out honorary Royal Ladies-in-Waiting sashes to eager children. "I, for one, won't stand and wait to see my kingdom repeatedly pillaged in this manner. It's time we take back the power.

"I've already told my fellow princesses that we will be meeting to discuss Enchantasia's welfare at a dinner my RLWs and I are organizing at Royal Manor this Friday. While commoners are usually not invited to give their opinion in such matters, I feel it is important that we hear everyone's thoughts on how to save our kingdom. One of my newest RLWs, Gillian Cobbler, is sure to have many ideas."

The village shoemaker's daughter and her friends are the ones who thwarted Alva's previous attack on FTRS. Inviting RLWs to a royal discussion is a bold move by Princess Rose, who has always let the other princesses make decisions on her behalf. "I am no longer willing to sit back and let things be decided for me. I'm a charming princess, yes, but I also have the power to help those in need."

Check your scrolls often throughout the day for updates on Enchantasia village and the search for Alva!

CHAPTER 14

A Pirate's Life for Me

Tap! Tap! Tap!

At first the sound is so light that I think I'm imagining it, so I roll over and go back to sleep. But the sound is persistent. It interrupts my sugarplum dreams.

Kayla throws back her covers. "For the love of fairies, what is that noise?"

The sun is not even close to gracing us with its presence, but someone is outside our turret window—and we live fourteen stories up. I rush over, open the stained glass window, and look out at the boy in pajamas sitting atop my favorite Pegasus, Macho. "Jax?"

"Hi," he says, sounding completely calm for someone who is breaking half a dozen FTRS rules by being outside, in the air, in the middle of the night, and stealing a Pegasus. After yesterday's attack on the village, Flora forbade us from even going outside. Macho's bright-white coat gleams almost silver in the moonlight, accentuating his majestic purple wings. "We need to powwow pronto. Ollie and Maxine think they've got something. Can you come outside?"

I look down, down, down at the ground so far below. The grounds are lit faintly by torches and an eerie silver glow that we suspect is Rumpelstiltskin's protection charm. "You want me to jump from my window onto Macho?" He nods like it's as easy as teaching one of the Three Blind Mice to swordfight (which Blackbeard is doing, by the way).

"Macho will hold steady, won't you?" Jax asks, and Macho neighs in response.

Pegasi can understand human thoughts and words, which I still find pretty cool.

"But he can't get closer." I stare at his large wingspan. "I'll have to jump."

Kayla nudges me out of the way and flies out the window, landing right behind Jax. She smiles smugly. "That was easy."

"Says the fairy with wings." I grab my boots, slipping them onto my bare feet. Then I hold up my nightgown, climb onto the small window ledge, and don't look down. Jax flies around again, getting as close as possible, which isn't all that close. I'm going to have to jump at least two to three feet.

"One, two, three," Jax coaxes me as Kayla clings to his back.

The air feels cool and it's breezier than I'd expected, but I take a deep breath and jump. Jax and Kayla have their hands out to catch me, and my hands are ready to meet theirs. *Whoosh!* A gust blows my nightgown up, and instinctively I pull it back down when I should be grabbing my friends' hands.

"Gilly!" Kayla screeches as I fall past Macho and plummet downward. I throw my hands out again, and at the last second they wind around Macho's loose reins. He gives a neigh in protest. "Would you rather I fall?" I ask him.

Jax grins. "We wouldn't have let you, thief. Macho clocks in at thirty miles an hour. We could have booked down and caught you before you went splat in the moat."

"Reassuring." I climb behind Kayla and hang on tight as Macho takes off, flying around the rooftop of the castle, which I've only seen once before. "So can you tell me what's so important that I needed to jump out a window?"

Jax's hair whips around his face as Macho flies, but his face darkens as a cloud blocks the moonlight. "Maxine received a new message on her scroll."

I yawn. "And she couldn't show it to us in the morning?"

"I forgot we haven't gotten you up to speed," Jax explains. "We're pretty sure the mole is one of the princesses."

"What?" I say and almost fall off Macho. His wing pushes me back on behind Kayla.

"The note Maxine got while you were off learning how to fold napkins said as much," says Kayla.

"And Maxine said this note is even more urgent," Jax explains, pulling Macho's reins tighter. The Pegasus soars to new heights. "We have to act now."

It's strange to see the castle bathed in darkness, the moat reflecting moonlight below while the occupants of FTRS are fast asleep. From high above, Fairy Tale Reform School looks peaceful. But we are anything but safe. Alva's army is growing. Two dozen students went missing after yesterday's attacks and many villagers as well. Alva's not going to stop 'til she has us all.

At least my family is safe. When we heard about the attack on the village, we feared the worst about Han and Hamish. Thankfully, Mother received word via magic carpet that the children at Mother Goose Nursery got to safety before the school was destroyed and our boot is still standing. "For now," Father said grimly. His words still echo in my head, along with the message on the threatening note he received. *Tell Gillian to be a charming girl and do what she's told.* I rub my arms to keep warm. If I want to end this, I may have to take the fall for all of us just like Harlow said. And if I do that, what will happen to my family?

Macho swoops down, going around the gardens and the observatory before he heads toward the lake. The sails of Blackbeard's ship billow in the breeze as Jax lands Macho on a freshly swabbed deck that gleams.

We've barely loosened our grips when scrappy-looking pirates come from every corner of the deck with swords drawn and shouting variations on "Aargh!" and "Avast! Intruders!" Jax is attempting to take off again when we hear someone yell, "Stop!"

Ollie runs across the deck, dressed like one of the crew in a bandana, billowy T-shirt, and ripped pantaloons. Maxine is with him. "They're with me, mates." The pirates seem disappointed as they put their swords back in their scabbards and go back to cleaning.

"Ollie, don't you think you're taking this pirate fantasy a bit far?" Kayla asks. "What are we doing here?"

"Once a pirate, always a pirate," says Ollie.

Blackbeard appears, putting an arm around Ollie. "This matey may not have sailed the seven seas with a pirate as fearsome as me, but I said I'd still invoke the pirate code and let ye meet on me decks." Blackbeard elbows Maxine. "I love this lad's tricks. Have you seen him make a dove appear under his hat? Bloody brilliant!" The other pirates applaud as Ollie bows. "Ye take all the time ye need, lad. I won't tell a soul."

Ollie and Blackbeard do a strange handshake and laugh before Blackbeard heads back to his quarters.

"Come and see the ship!" Ollie tells us excitedly, lifting a hatch in the deck to reveal steps that lead to the quarters below. "We're safe from prying eyes here so it's the perfect place to talk before the sun comes up." He pauses. "As long as Gilly has her rose pin and sash off."

I point to my blue nightgown. "I'm good. But why the need to meet outside the castle?"

Ollie leads the way down. "We're trying to keep tabs on you! The girls told us what you overheard yesterday."

"We figured news like that would probably make you do something rash and thiefy on your own," Jax adds.

"I've learned my lesson about working alone," I say, exhaling at the thought of it all. "We're only going to be able to stop Alva if we work as a team, even if she is only after me."

Jax stops near a room filled with snoring pirates in hammocks. "We won't let her take you. We can stop her together. *All* of us." Jax opens a door where Jocelyn is waiting.

CHAPTER 15

Riddle Me This

ᔔᔕ

She's helping us?" I flip out. "You just said you heard her sister wants to hand me over to Alva!"

"She didn't actually say that," Jocelyn scoffs. "But it's true that sometimes sacrifices have to be made." Jax holds me back while Kayla blocks Jocelyn.

"Have you all lost your minds?" I hiss. "Harlow is working with Flora and Alva, which means Blackbeard probably is too. You're trusting villains, and villains can't be trusted. Jocelyn included!"

Jocelyn crosses her arms, showing off the intricate pattern of her black lace sleeves. "She's as pigheaded as the Three Little Pigs. She'll never listen to anything I have to say. You deserve to have your boot blown down!"

Jax steps between us. "Enough! Alva's taking students and villagers, and Enchantasia and FTRS will be next. Do you want that to happen?" He looks from me to Jocelyn. We're both quiet. "Now, there's no one better to decipher villainous clues than the sister of the Evil Queen. Jocelyn's figured out how to work the manifestos on her own, and she's willing to help us sort through these clues, so we're going to let her."

I've never heard Jax so fired up before. I rub my sore arm and glare at Jocelyn. "I have one question first: Why do you want to help us?"

Jocelyn purses her purplish lips. "I think my sister is innocent." I snort. "I think Harlow left with Alva because she's secretly helping FTRS. Maybe she's even the one clever enough to send these notes. Did you ever think of that?"

I snicker. "Yeah. And poison apples aren't really poisonous."

The wind picks up in the room, and Jocelyn begins to mumble what I suspect is a spell. I lunge for her. The two of us hit a sack of what must be gold coins—it's that hard—and both wince. "Ow! Ow!" we both exclaim.

Ollie and Jax send us to opposite sides of the room. "You two are not allowed to talk to each other," Jax says wearily. "Let's fill Gilly in on what we know. Jocelyn?"

Jocelyn huffs, then finally looks at me. "All those fools who joined Alva yesterday? They did it by touching the manifesto."

"Those scrolls are protected," I snap. "You can't pull one down or touch it." Jax gives me a warning look. I back down with a sigh. "Can you?"

"You can if you're questionable," Jocelyn insists. "I've been hanging around the manifesto to see if anyone tries to use it. After yesterday's attack, students flocked to it."

"Traitors," Ollie grumbles.

"Most of them got nowhere," Jocelyn explains with an eye roll. "They were too reformed, I guess, but then that weasel Ronald Gertrude, who keeps trying to sneak off with Pegasi on school grounds, went up to it, and the scroll changed color."

"Ronald?" Maxine's eye starts to spin. "What a boy who cried wolf! His mother has been trying to spring him from FTRS early!"

"That little troll walked up to the manifesto with two friends, stuck a meaty hand on it, and begged to join Alva." Jocelyn snickers. "New words appeared but I was too far away to read them. When Ronald escaped through the castle wall, I went over to try the scroll myself." She shrugs. "If you're still evil enough, it reveals itself." She holds out her hand, and the purple smoke I'm used to seeing with her magic reveals words. The handwriting matches Alva's manifesto.

Meet at the Hollow Woods at dawn. Our Royal Manor battle is imminent.

Dawn? I look through the nearest porthole and see the sky is already turning pink. "Fiddlesticks! We're too late to stop them!"

"We may not be able to keep them from joining Alva, but we can figure out which princess is aiding her." Jax holds out a scribbled note. "This was what Maxine's last note said: 'The traitor is of royal blood, for sure, but the question remains, which tiara is tarnished?'"

I listen to the snoring in the other room to steady myself. I've never been a royal fan, and I certainly don't like how they've abandoned FTRS, but I never thought a princess would stoop so low as to work with Alva. "Who do you think would betray Enchantasia?"

"We don't know." Maxine pulls out her mini magical scroll. "But tonight I got this." We all gather around to look. "It glowed so brightly that it woke me up. It says 'Urgent.'"

> HEAR MY CRY! THE TIME HAS COME! YOU MUST
> WORK FAST! THE ROYAL SPY IS ALMOST FREE
> AT LAST. HER HAIR IS FAIR, HER SKIN IS WHITE.
> SADLY, I KNOW SHE IS NOT SNOW WHITE.

"Well, that rules out one princess, but we still have three more," Jax says. He spreads the notes and Maxine's mini magical scroll out in front of us on the messy pirate table, pushing aside maps and gold telescopes. "Any ideas when they're all blond?"

"Ella would never do such a thing," says Maxine fiercely. "She's always speaking out on evil. I just can't imagine her trying to hurt the kingdom."

"Well, it can't be Rose either," I insist. "She's working at FTRS! She believes in reform and helping the kingdom. She's always complaining the court doesn't do more to help bring power to the people."

"I'm with Gilly," says Maxine. "Princess Rose officially made me an RLW yesterday! She said if Gilly wants me in the club, then I'm in the club. I was so thankful that I tried to bring her my secret stash of gingerroot flowers."

"You have gingerroot?" We all freak, and I hear the pirates in the next cabin stir.

Ollie is aghast. "That flower is a hotter commodity than radishes for dealing with beasties. Why would you just give it away?"

Maxine's left side of her face starts to droop. "I still have it. Princess Rose took one look at it and started backing away."

"Duh!" Jocelyn says. "She was surrounded by gingerroot during her Sleeping Beauty phase."

I pat Maxine on the back. "I'm sure she appreciated the effort. But that means if it's not Snow, Ella, or Rose…" We all look at Jax.

His violet eyes nearly bulge out of his head. "You think it's Rapunzel? She would never try to hurt Enchantasia!"

"And you know that how?" Jocelyn asks, examining a nail. "From the way Kayla tells it, Prince, you haven't seen your sis in years, going incognito and all."

Kayla blushes. "I had to bring her up to speed."

"You said Rapunzel was there when the gargoyles attacked Royal Manor," Ollie says quietly. "And *HEAS* says she was in the village right before the attacks yesterday too."

"Not to mention the extra-long blond hair I found on a threatening note Father received at Cobbler Shoes," I add gently.

"What?" Kayla gasps.

I stare at a gold telescope on the cluttered table. "It basically said if I didn't do as I was told—whatever that means—Father's business could be taken away." I look at the others. "But Father's right. I can't just worry about my family. I have to think of all of us, and my gut tells me that Rapunzel is the mole."

Jax sits down, dumbfounded. "You guys really think the traitor is my sister? Father sent me undercover at FTRS, and the whole time the mole was my own sister? I just don't believe it."

And yet, I think he does. It makes the most sense out of the three princesses. The boat sways gently, and we all grab a chair as we look at each other in fear.

"Maybe she's planning to steal the crown from the other princesses and Alva and keep it all to herself," Jocelyn guesses, and we look at her. "That's what I would do."

Kayla's wings disappear and she drops down to the ground, seemingly deflated. "Guys, if we're right, no one will believe Rapunzel is working with Alva. Not Flora, not the Dwarf Police Squad."

"I could get word to Father," Jax says miserably, "but I'm not sure he would believe me either, especially without proof. This is a conversation I need to have with him in person and that's impossible since he's away trying to deal with this ogre mess."

"So let's follow our hunch and see if we're right," I say. "We can confront her on our own."

"School be starting soon, buckaroos!" Blackbeard bellows from above. "Best to be getting this Pegasus home. The sea is no place for a flying horse." I hear the pirates begin stirring and calling out orders.

Jax still looks dazed. "How do we do that?"

"You guys will join me at the royal dinner Rose is throwing," I decide there and then. "She already invited me, and Maxine will get an invite too since she's an RLW now. We can go and try to talk some sense into Rapunzel. Jax, she may not know you, but you are her brother. Maybe she'll listen. Lock her away and make her!"

"The rest of us will be on guard for Alva," says Jocelyn.

"A dinner with all the princesses and village guests would be the perfect place for her to make her move and snatch Gilly. I would do that." I glare at her.

"You guys have all this worked out when all we have is a hunch?" Kayla sinks into a big pirate chair.

"Come on, guys!" Maxine rallies. "We've done this before. We just need to stick together and maybe use my gingerroot." She pulls the smushed flowers out of her pocket. "I'm glad I didn't give these to Rose now."

"Hold on to them," Jax suggests, smiling weakly. I feel bad. Learning your sister is evil is not easy to swallow. "We're going to need them."

I look at the group before me. A pirate, an ogre, a witch, a fairy, a royal, and me. These aren't good odds, but maybe Father and Maxine are right: together, we can do anything.

I smile. "Yes. Let's show these villains they've got nothing on our crew."

From the Official Stationery of the Royal Court of Enchantasia*

Princess Ella, Princess Snow, Princess Rapunzel, and Princess Rose

Gillian Cobbler

is officially invited to a dinner meeting at Royal Manor this Thursday evening. You may bring guests!

Dinner hosted by Princess Rose and the Royal Ladies-in-Waiting Club of Fairy Tale Reform School.

*Write like a royal! Order your own royal-looking stationery today at the royal court gift shop. (Please note: It is not official and cannot be used to issue orders.)

Please be prepared for a security briefing by the Dwarf Police Squad led by Chief Pete. Royal meetings are not taken lightly in these times!

Dinner will consist of roast beef and figgy pudding, but the royal court does not discriminate based on palate or breed. For alternate magical creature options, please contact our chef, Patacake BakersMan, by Pegasus Post.

Does your guest want to be a Royal Lady-in-Waiting? Do you have what it takes? Contact Princess Rose for a meeting at her office at Fairy Tale Reform School today!

CHAPTER 16

To the Castle We Go

I have one foot in the Pegasi carriage when I hear Miri loud and clear. "Gillian Cobbler, you must halt by order of Headmistress Flora!" The mirror in the Pegasi stables is flashing red, which is a very bad sign.

I point innocently to myself and glance quickly back at my friends and Jocelyn, who shrugs. "But I haven't done anything wrong." *Like lock up a princess to protect our kingdom. Yet.*

"The headmistress would like a word," Miri says. "She's on her way now."

"Mind if we jump ahead of you, Gilly?" Azalea asks uneasily. She and Dahlia were in line behind us, but at the mention of their mother, they push their way forward, their heavy perfume making Maxine sneeze. Both girls are wearing poufy ball gowns in different shades of purple with their new RLW sashes. Azalea grabs Dahlia's hand, yanks her sister into the carriage, and rushes the driver to take off. "Don't mention you saw us or our new glass-slipper high tops, okay?"

Their flight takes off seconds before Flora opens the stable doors. Professor Wolfington is with her and seems calm, but Flora's mood is stormy. The look on her face makes the stable boys dive out of her path. Macho neighs nervously from his stable.

Don't worry, boy, I say, knowing he can hear my thoughts.

"Did you not get my note?" asks Headmistress Flora sharply, and the rest of my crew steps back.

"The one that said, 'I'd rather you not go to the dinner'?" I ask innocently, playing with the gold thread in the dress Mother sent me for the meeting. I sent back the glass-slipper high tops. I prefer my boots. My hair is pulled into an updo that highlights the purple stripe in my hair. It's kind of growing on me. "It seemed more like a request than a demand."

The growl that comes next sounds like it could be from Professor Wolfington, but it's still Flora. "Under the circumstances of what's happening in Enchantasia, I do not feel it is wise for students to leave the grounds. I cannot protect you if you're not in my care."

"Seems like you're not doing a great job of protecting us here either," I say and Maxine pinches me. Her fingers are pudgy so it hurts! But she's right. I can't be snippy or Flora might realize I overheard her talking to Harlow.

Flora's face hardens. "This dinner is poor timing. I have a very bad feeling about tonight. You were lucky last time, but who is to say your luck won't run out if you encounter Alva again?" Macho neighs again softly. "You have to trust that we're doing everything we can to stop her. We're working with people like Rumpel. I never thought I'd speak with him again unless he agreed to a transformation under our care, and yet here we are." Her eyes are pleading. "Let us do what we need to bring that fairy in and then you'll be safe to visit Royal Manor another time." I say nothing.

"I'd go, but no one can enter Royal Manor without an invitation. Strangely, Princess Rose did not give any to the FTRS staff," Professor Wolfington adds, and I notice he's staring at me and Jax intently. "I guess our opinion on Alva isn't warranted."

"We'll bring you back a souvenir," Ollie says. "I hear the silverware is solid gold. One spoon could buy the school a Pegasus."

Headmistress Flora sounds flustered. "Oliver, this is no time for follies! Now I cannot tell you all to ignore a royal invitation, but I *strongly* suggest you do so. I forbade my own daughters to attend tonight under the circumstances."

"Uh, you might want to go check on them in their quarters," Kayla suggests. "And look for new glass-slipper high-top boxes too." Flora's nostrils flare.

I feel ill and I don't think it's that extra pot pie I had at lunch with Maxine. I think Flora is hinting that we might not make it back from Royal Manor. What does she care? Isn't she working with Harlow to get rid of me to save our school? I glance at Jax and know we can't wait to find out what Flora is really up to. This isn't just about my safety. It's about our whole kingdom's, including the royals. Like it or not, I have to go.

"I'm sorry, Headmistress Flora," I say. "Madame Cleo told me it's uncharming of a proper lady to ignore an invitation from a royal."

"Fine! But remember, I can do nothing for you from

here." Flora stomps off and stable boys dive out of the way again, but Professor Wolfington stays behind. He's chomping on a piece of straw between his lips, studying me closely.

"Sir?" Jax sounds very proper. He looks regal in a white dress suit, gold buttons lining his chest.

"The headmistress is right that we cannot protect you if you're not on the grounds, but I believe there's something she forgot to mention." His eyes are almost playful. "Different castle, different rules. You can't get in trouble for breaking FTRS codes of conduct if the staff is not there to see it happen." His eyes glimmer. "Princess Rose is not a teacher; she's a club advisor. Understood?"

Is he trying to say it's okay to be bad tonight? I'm not sure, but I nod anyway.

"Good. Then I bid you a good evening," he says. "I also have a gift." He pulls a small velvet sack out of his jacket pocket. "Gingerroot. It can bind magic. I believe Miss Maxine has been growing some in her dorm room for a rainy day, but my batch is already mature. Extra might come in handy this evening."

I hold out my hand in wonderment. Maybe Wolfington

really is one of the good guys. "Thank you," I say, tucking the bag into my small clutch.

"Mine is mature too. I *think*," Maxine mumbles in my ear, blowing hot breath on me.

"Gingerroot is great, but it only works a short while," Wolfington adds. "Use it at the last possible second. You'll have fifteen minutes to a half hour if it's potent enough."

"The next carriage is approaching," a stable boy informs us, and two Pegasi swoop down with a golden carriage attached behind them. They land outside the stable doors.

"Guess we should go," says Kayla, sounding anxious as she takes Ollie's arm and heads toward the carriage. With a nod to the professor, I take Jax's arm while Maxine and Jocelyn walk together.

"Ready, thief?" Jax asks.

"I guess I have to be." I step up into the carriage and sit down on one of the velvet seats. This is the first time I've traveled by carriage. Well, if you don't count our return trip from the village in the carriage trunk. Somehow I suspect this trip will be just as rocky—in a different way.

* * *

"Announcing our royal guest, Miss Gillian Cobbler of 2 Boot Way!"

Having passed through security with Pete, who seemed none too pleased to see me, we are escorted into the castle compound where I'm announced like royalty.

I hate to admit it, but Royal Manor is pretty impressive. From my view in the village, I couldn't tell that there were actually four castles inside the main gate—one for each princess—and a fifth central castle used for hosting lavish balls and princess meetings. When we flew overhead, we could really see how differently each princess had modeled her castle. Ella's is made of glass like her slipper; Snow's is hand-carved wood (said to be designed by her adoring dwarfs); and Rapunzel's is the most modern with pictures of her latest hair-care ads projected onto the white stucco walls. Rose's is covered with rose-covered ivy that climbs to the tallest turret.

"Isn't it enchanting?" Maxine gushes, clutching her RLW sash. She looks at me and frowns. "Where's your sash? Princess Rose sent it over to the dorms last night in a lovely rose-scented box."

"Maxine, have you hit your head? They have trackers in

them," Jocelyn hisses as we make our way along the receiving line.

Maxine clutches hers in horror. "That's not true. Tessa told me Headmistress Flora made Rose take them out."

"So you're wearing that thing for fun?" Jocelyn snickers. "I'd rather be eaten by a wolf than wear that sash."

Knowing what I know now, I kind of agree. That makes two times I've agreed with Jocelyn in the last few days. The stress of this Alva business must be getting to me.

Maxine pouts. "I've always wanted an RLW sash. I can't give it up now!"

Jocelyn rolls her eyes and steps forward to shake hands with the first of the princes. I watch his face as he realizes who is before him. The young witch dressed all in black is easily recognizable as Harlow's sister, but he treats her like any other guest, as does Snow. Kayla and Maxine, who are next in line, drool over Rapunzel and Ella, who have the most spectacular gowns I've ever seen. Ella's sparkles like diamonds. I don't see Rose, but I guess she's busy getting ready for our dinner meeting.

Ella takes my hand in hers. "I'm glad I finally got the chance to meet you in person, Gillian. I wish it were under better circumstances, but I'm still glad you're here," she says in a wispy voice as her tiny hand holds my own. I can't get over all her rings and the jewels on her wrist. "We owe so much to you and your bravery. Your family must be so proud of all you've done for Enchantasia."

"Thank you, Princess Ella." I am astonished. We move along and Maxine shakes Ella's hand fiercely, but I can't stop thinking of the compliment I just received. *I haven't done it alone*, says a little voice in my head, and that makes me feel sheepish. Look at Jax. He's has been undercover for years, never getting glory, never getting to go to royal family dinners or have Rapunzel know his true identity, all to help his kingdom. Now he has to take on his own sister! Me? All I've done with the hero title is watch my family reap the reward and let others heap praise on me.

I interrupt Ella and Maxine's conversation. "Princess? I appreciate the praise, but what the people don't seem to realize is that my bravery was only made possible because it was part of a group effort." I look at Jax and Maxine. "My friends are stronger than I could ever be. They did just as much if not more to save our school. I wish they could get the same recognition." Maxine is so flabbergasted that drool puddles in her mouth. Jax's royal mouth practically hits the floor.

"That's lovely of you to commend your friends," Princess Ella says, surveying me closely. "Please be sure to take a gift bag on your way into the dining hall. It's full of Rapunzel's latest hair-care products, one of which benefits the Three Blind Mice Charity, plus a discount card for my new favorite salon, Molly Whuppie."

"What was that about?" Jax asks as we breeze through introductions with Snow White without incident. "Are you going soft?"

"I just want you guys to get credit for your part in all this too." I hear a string quartet begin to play something dinner worthy in the next room. I look at the tips of my trusty boots. "I'm sorry I've been so selfish."

Jax pops a treat in his mouth from a waiter rushing to the ballroom. "We would have knocked that chip off your shoulder eventually. Or Jocelyn would have."

"Here we go!" Ollie whispers as we approach Rapunzel. He pulls a deck of cards out of his pocket. "I'm going to impress Rapunzel to get her attention. Jax, you follow me and try to pull her away."

At Jax's sister's name, I feel him tense up. He hasn't been in the same room with her in years. (She was locked in that tower and then was told her brother was at boarding school when she moved into Royal Manor.) Their father also charmed Rapunzel's memories so any image she has of him is distorted. She *shouldn't* recognize him, but knowing what we know now, I am worried.

I open my mouth to express my concern and find Jax already bowing before his sister. "My princess, it's so lovely of you to invite the students of Fairy Tale Reform School to dinner this evening. I'm Jax Porter, and this, as you know, is Gillian Cobbler." I quickly curtsy. This time I don't fall. *RLW class is working! Woot!*

"Jax, what a pleasure," Rapunzel says, clearly impressed by his royal dress and speech. "Although I must admit, the invitation was not mine." She frowns ever so slightly. "Princess Rose was insistent we invite you all this evening. The rest of us were very concerned about safety with everything going on, but I guess we do have the Dwarf Police Squad here." Her eyes move toward Olaf and ours follow. He's eating one of the floral arrangements. Those guys are going to be a *huge* help tonight.

"Well, I look forward to discussing the matter with you, Princess," Jax says smoothly. "If you have a moment, I'd love to talk about how Fairy Tale Reform School is fairing under Alva's threat. The students are worried about ogre attacks."

Rapunzel clears her throat, but it sounds more like a squeak. Her blond hair is in a side braid that is woven with flowers and drapes around her neck like a scarf. "Absolutely," she says. "Although I dare say ogres are usually peaceful when they aren't under Alva's rule." She sighs. "We will talk more after I finish this receiving line."

Yes! Jax is in.

"Smooth," I say as a page hands us gift bags with Rapunzel's latest hair-care ad sketched on the side. I peek into the bag and see shampoo, conditioner, and detangler, along with a purple detangling brush. There is also a bar of chocolate that smells divine. Anna will flip over this stuff, and the boys will love the chocolate. I wonder if I can get a few extra bars. We watch as the page nervously gives Jocelyn two instead of one.

"Come on, guest of honor." Jax offers me his arm and walks me along the pink carpet to the ballroom. The others are already inside. "Let's scout out this overthrow—I mean, party. Wait 'til you get a load of this place."

"Jax, it's just a ballroom. I've seen them before." In

Happily Ever After Scrolls. But when a page opens the doors for us, I inhale sharply. "Whoa."

"Told you so," Jax brags.

The Royal Manor ballroom is as big as the village—and I'm not exaggerating. I can't see from one end to the other with all the large rose arrangements on the tables. Some of the RLWs are already seated at a long table with napkins folded like roses (nice touch), confetti, and enough candles to light a whole boot. There is even a narrow upper level filled with thrones of every shape, size, and color that overlook a gold-and-white dance floor lit by the largest candelabra I've ever seen. Where is Jocelyn? I want to keep my eyes on her. The others may trust her completely, but I still have my doubts. Tessa, Olivia, and Raza are dancing in the middle of the floor already, while Ollie, Kayla, and Maxine ogle the plates and silverware. They must be solid gold.

For a moment, I feel a familiar pang of longing. Just one or two forks would feed my family for months. But no! That's not why I'm here.

"I wonder where Rose is," I whisper to Jax. "Do you think I should tell her about Rapunzel?"

Jax raises an eyebrow. "No. We need definite proof. Let's

make sure we have the right princess before you go blabbing to everyone else. Let me talk to Rapunzel first."

"Gift bag?" Raza sees us and runs over, practically throwing a bright-pink tulle bag at each of us. "It's got rose-flavored chocolates inside. Don't they smell divine?" Jax sneezes. "Bless you! They're delicious. Far nicer than the royal court gift-bag chocolates."

She looks at my purple gift bag with disdain, and I wish I had hid it behind my back. I'm not parting with it. "Princess Rose is hurt that the royal court gave out a separate gift bag," Raza says. "This dinner meeting was her idea after all. The rest of the court didn't want us here."

Jax blows his nose with a handkerchief. "The princesses run the kingdom. They should keep us informed, but we shouldn't be privy to their discussions."

Raza glares at him while she adjusts her sash. "Princess Rose says her reign is an open book. We can ask her anything we want. Unlike the other princesses who are always looking down their noses at her."

"Jackson?" Rapunzel calls Jax by his formal name and he tenses up. "Princess Rose would like us all to be honorary Ladies-in-Waiting tonight." She whips her butt-length hair behind her head. "She says she has sashes for all of us to wear. Would you be so kind as to help me find them? I figured we could have a chat while we search."

My heart beats wildly. I don't want Jax going off alone with Rapunzel. "I'll join you."

"It's all right. I'll help the princess," Jax insists, his violet eyes trying to convey some sort of message. "Don't wander off. I'll be right back."

"But…" How can I stay here when Jocelyn is out there doing who knows what? What is she up to? We were supposed to stay together! I head over to Ollie and Maxine to see if they know anything. "Jax just left with Rapunzel."

"Flapjacks, that was quick," Ollie says. "I guess we'll know her true colors soon enough. Should one of us shadow him?"

I shake my head. "I don't think he wanted to be followed. It could raise suspicion. Speaking of which, have any of you seen Jocelyn?"

Ollie pales. "I thought she was with you."

Something is definitely up. "I'll pop out and find her."

"There will be no popping!" scolds one of the RLWs, coming up behind us. "Princess Rose said to keep you here." Maxine's bad eye begins to roll. "The dinner portion of the meeting will be starting shortly." The girl tries to lead us all to the table and place me in the head seat. I have to think fast.

"But I'm nervous!" I lie. "My hair needs a touchup, and my lips just aren't pink enough for the occasion."

"You look lovely." The girl looks me over. "Although your nose is shiny."

"Very shiny," I agree. "I'll touch up before Princess Rose joins us. Do you want to go with me to the loo?" Maxine looks ready to say yes when the others sigh.

"A proper lady never announces she's going to the bathroom or invites others to join her," says a fairy named Ariana. "You say, 'I must powder my nose.'"

I feign embarrassment. "I have to powder my nose. Anyone know where the loo is?"

Ariana's cheeks burn. "The *powder room* in the Royal Chambers is closest, but there was a water leak in there. I can take you to one in another hall. I'm supposed to escort you anywhere outside this room so you don't get lost. Shall we?"

Water leak in the main bathroom, huh? No one will go in there unless they're hiding something. Or someone. I wonder if that's what Jocelyn was thinking too. "I'm fine," I insist as

Ariana tries to follow. Thankfully a waiter with a large platter of beef cuts her off. "I'll be right back."

"Gift bag?" a page asks as I rush out of the ballroom.

Oh, what the heck. I take a second one since I left my first one on my seat inside. Now I have more chocolate! "Thanks! Royal Chamber is this way, right?" The page nods. I hurry as fast as this heavy gown will let me go 'til I find the sign I'm looking for. *Royal Court—Held by Princesses Ella, Snow, Rapunzel, and Rose.*

I pull at the door and find it locked. Thankfully I've got bobby pins to spare in this updo Maxine gave me. I pull one out just as I hear footsteps approaching. Pulling the pin apart so that it is one long piece, I stick it in the lock and poke around 'til I hear the click. The door opens and I slip inside just as I hear a page walk by whistling, "Hey Diddle Diddle."

There are no lights inside the chamber, but I can make out the four thrones on a pedestal at the front of the room. I walk to the front railing and lean over, imagining what I would come here to ask for. I know Father came once to ask for his glass slipper patent and was denied. That only made me dislike the royals more, and yet after what happened at FTRS, they brought Father here to give him his job back.

What we did at school not only saved his business, but also changed my family's life. If I fail today, Alva won't just take the shoe business; she'll take everything. I shudder and that's when I hear the whispering. Light is coming from under the doorway to the private chambers. There is only one word I need to hear before I burst through the door. "Gillian."

I crash right into Jocelyn, who is holding hands with exactly who I suspected. Her sister. Harlow is wearing her finest Evil Queen regalia—a purple cape that has a collar so high it hits her ears. "You!" I point to Jocelyn. "I knew you couldn't be trusted! You're working with her."

Jocelyn's eyes widen. "Gilly. Wait. You have this wrong. Harlow explained everything." She tries to take my hand and I shake her off. "Don't act like Humpty Dumpty! We don't have much time. You have to—"

"Why would I listen to a villain?" I interrupt.

The Evil Queen moves out of the shadows and I get a glimpse of her polished, made-up face. Her black dress glistens with silver crystals that make me blink. Exile has not diminished Harlow's ability to look polished. Or scary. Her lips curl into a familiar scowl. "You foolish girl. We are your only hope and time is running out." She holds out her hand. "Come with me now and we'll explain everything."

"Come with you?" I laugh. They must think I've lost my mind. "Never!" I slowly pull the velvet bag Wolfington gave me out of my pocket, but Harlow spots it.

"Do not waste that gingerroot on me!" Harlow commands. Jocelyn lungs for the bag, but I climb onto a long table so Jocelyn can't reach me.

Jocelyn quickly climbs on after me. "Stop running! Cobbler, you're going to cause your own doom! Listen to my sister!"

"Never!" I open the small bag and look quickly at the roots and petals in the bag. There's no way I can tie the roots around Harlow's wrists. She'll stop me. The petals don't work as long, but it's the only shot I have to get away. "A leopard doesn't change its spots." I repeat the words I've heard Harlow say before.

Harlow's laugh is long and throaty. "And you are so reformed, missy?" Harlow inches closer. I can feel Jocelyn closing in from the other side. "Think, peasant. What is your head telling you?"

"I may be a thief—some would even call me a

villain—but even I am smart enough not to trust a witch." As Jocelyn reaches for the bag, I open it and blow the petals into the air. Within seconds, the Evil Queen and her little sister are frozen.

I breathe a sigh of relief.

That's when I hear someone clapping.

"Nicely done, Miss Gillian," says Princess Rose, emerging from the shadows and smiling warmly. "You've saved the day again! Capturing the Evil Queen and her sister! Such a hero you are. How will we honor you this time?"

"Princess Rose!" I say breathlessly. "Forget honors! We don't have much time. The traitor in the castle is a princess. I think Rapunzel is working with Alva." Her brow furrows and I worry that Jax is right—I shouldn't knock a princess to a fellow princess—but Rose is kind. She could help us. "We have to stop her before she lets Alva in the castle."

Rose purses her lips. "I think it's too late for that." She gently pries the gingerroot bag from my hands, but I don't understand what she's doing. Rose opens the bag and pulls out the roots. "She's already here," she whispers in my ear.

I feel my throat begin to constrict. "She is? Where?" I whirl around to reach the door. "We have to warn the others!"

Something zaps me in the back and my legs feel like they're on fire. I fall to the ground and see Rose standing over me with the gingerroot stems in her hands. She leans down and begins to tie them around my wrists. The stems are stronger than just the roots and leave me soundless.

"Gillian, it pains me to do this to you," Rose says calmly as she ties the roots around me. I may not have magic, but I can be frozen. I feel the tingling spread from my fingertips to my toes. I try to move and can't. I want to scream. Warn Jax and the others. *We were wrong! It's not Rapunzel! It's Rose.* But I'm too late.

Rose shushes me like a baby to calm me. "I like you. I really do." Her blue eyes narrow as she strokes my forehead. "But I like having power more." Her face comes close to mine and I can smell her rose-scented perfume. She smiles sinisterly. "Now let's hand you over to Alva so I can take control of the kingdom."

CHAPTER 17

Every Rose Has Its Thorn

I struggle to move, willing my body to wake up, but it doesn't. I can feel the tingling, but I can't speak, I can't lift my pinkie, and I can't scream. I'm all alone with the mole and I'm trapped. I feel like such a fool. We picked the wrong princess. How could I not have seen this coming? The obsession with power? The way Rose threatened me to join the RLWs? She must have been the one who sent that note to Father too.

Princess Rose uses a wand to lift my body off the table and bring it slowly toward the open doorway where she is waiting.

"I'm sorry it had to be like this," she says coolly as I begin to glide out of the private chambers and into the courtroom again. "I liked you. Truly I did. You have fire! You are stubborn, yes, and willful!" She laughs to herself. "But I thought you'd make a wonderful second-in-command under my reign. Alas, Alva wants you to pay the price for interfering in her affairs, and I cannot mess up the agreement we already made." She shrugs her bare shoulders and I can hear the red gown she's wearing swish. "Alva will do away with you and rule somewhere far, far away, and then I'll get my kingdom all to myself. Your life is a small price for me to pay."

My body begins to rotate and I catch glimpses of Rose. She taps a mirror and the glass begins to swirl 'til I see a face on the other side. "Yes?" I hear Alva's smooth voice.

Rose curtsies. "It's done, Wicked One. I have the girl."

"Good! I'll come out of hiding. Bring her to the ballroom for all to see."

"But, the others. Gillian's friends will try to stop us." Rose sounds anxious.

Alva laughs. "Foolish little princess. Now that we have the hero, the others will easily fall. Go. Before I change my mind on this deal."

"Yes, Wicked One." Rose curtsies. When the mirror darkens, Rose uses her wand to guide me out the doorway and down the castle hall. "She doesn't have to be so bossy about everything," Rose mumbles. "We're supposed to be partners. I infiltrate FTRS and build her army, she scares the people into wanting a regime change, and *voila*! I get my kingdom all to myself.

"You have no idea how hard it is to get a say when three other princesses always think they're wiser. It's a nightmare! 'Rose, you're too busy pruning roses to read a scroll and know what's going on in the kingdom!'" she mimics. "'Rose, if you paid more attention to the villagers' complaints and less to what tailor you want to move into the kingdom, you'd know why we need to have a Dwarf Police Squad.'" She moans. "Ella, Rapunzel, and Snow think they know everything!"

My eyes dart around the hallway, which is quiet. Everyone must be in the ballroom by now. I hear the music playing and the sounds of talking and laughter. A waiter appears in a doorway and yelps when he sees us, but he doesn't get far. Rose gives a zap with her wand and he's immobilized.

"Now that Enchantasia is about to become mine, I can do anything I want with the kingdom and make it so much better like…like…" She stops for a moment and bites her full lips. "Well, I'm not sure what I'll do, but I'm sure whatever it is will be wonderful!"

Rose zaps open the ballroom doors and sends me gliding through them onto the main table. People scream and jump up as my body slides along the dishes and glasses, knocking things to the floor until I come to a halt in front of Ella and Snow.

"Dinner is served!" Rose says with a laugh.

The caramel cake in Ollie's mouth falls out.

"What have you done to Gilly?" Maxine cries. Rose zaps a water glass near Maxine's hand and it splatters water everywhere.

Snow waves her Dwarf Police Squad over, but Rose zaps them too and they freeze in mid-run. "Sister, what are you doing?"

"What I should have done a long time ago!" Rose cries. "I'm tired of being the one princess with no power. I want a chance to rule!"

"You're the one always off dancing in the forest instead of coming to meetings," Snow mumbles.

Ella remains seated. "Rose, unbind this poor girl and we'll discuss this calmly and privately in our chambers. You can't be so rash!"

"*No!*" Rose says hotly and I see her knuckles tighten. "I'm tired of not getting a say. When word came that my former captor was still out there wreaking havoc, did you rush to find her? No! You let the rest of the kingdom deal with her. No one helps me! So now I'll help myself. Wicked One! Come and claim your prize!"

Alva glides through the ballroom door with her gargoyles, and I feel my heartbeat rev up. It's about the only thing I can feel, although my fingers are starting to tingle. The party guests scream as Alva walks straight to the head of the table where I lie. "At last! I have the little troublemaker!" When Alva leans over me, I see her dark-red gown, pointy cape, and jet-black hair swept up in a high bun adorned with jewels that scream *villain*. Her smile soon fades. "Seize them all!" Alva tells the gargoyles, flipping her cape and walking away from the table.

Several of the RLWs dive under tables and chairs or take off for the second-floor balcony. They don't get far from the dozens of gargoyles that screech and hiss as they fly around the room grabbing RLWs and invited guests. But three people run toward the gargoyles to get closer to me—Kayla, Ollie, and Maxine.

"I don't think I've ever seen Gilly hold still this long," Ollie cracks.

"Ollie!" Kayla reprimands as Maxine swats a gargoyle

away with a gold plate that it takes off with instead. "We have to help her. How do we stop the gingerroot effects?"

"You can't. They have to wear off." Maxine reaches a hand for me, and my body sways slightly. I could swear my left leg moved, but I can't seem to get it going again. "We could hide her somewhere 'til they do." She pulls my dress toward her and my body glides to my friends. I think I feel Maxine push on my chest and lower me beneath the table. "She'll be safe under here."

"Will we all be safe?" Ollie asks, ducking down with a caramel cake in his hand. A gargoyle snatches it. "Hey! That was mine!"

"We got this all wrong!" Maxine cries. "I can't believe Princess Rose is the traitor, not Rapunzel! Speaking of which, where is she? And Jax? Or Jocelyn? Where did everyone go?" Her good eye widens. "Do you think Rose captured them too?"

Dinner plates crash off the tables around us. "I don't know! I just saw Pete and Olaf dragged off to the second-floor balcony," Ollie says. "People are running in terror. We have to get word to Flora."

Maxine finds a piece of glass. "Will this reach Miri?"

"Good thinking!" Kayla says and pulls a training wand

from her pocket. She's obviously stolen it from school. "Let there be light!" she shouts. The wand illuminates briefly, then flashes red. "Illegal use of magic!" Miri says.

"Miri!" The others hover around the shard of glass in Maxine's hands.

"My heavens! What is that screeching?" Miri asks, but her voice is drowned out as a gargoyle yanks the tablecloth above us off our table and sends everyone scurrying. In the chaos, Maxine drops the glass and it shatters. I definitely felt a shard hit my leg. The spell is lifting! My legs are tingling now and so are my arms.

"Princesses, it's so nice to see you all wrapped up like a present," I hear Alva say. I see her shoes heading toward us. Maxine pulls my body closer, and this time I'm certain I can feel her touching my side!

"She's got them boxed in a corner with the gargoyles surrounding them," Ollie reports in a whisper. "Should I throw some radishes?"

"No, they'll see you! Wait 'til the coast is clear and we'll get Gilly out of here before Alva spots her," Kayla suggests. I'm loving how she's taking charge. "We'll come back in to save the others somehow."

"Mrwrh," I say. My lips are moving!

"She's coming out of it!" Maxine whispers. "She's moving! Her arm is moving! Her—" I wiggle around, still floating under Rose's spell. I'm still hovering. "She's back! Sort of."

"I can fix that," Kayla says and flicks the wand at me. I fall into Maxine's lap.

"Wrong," I say in between short breaths. "Mistake. Rose. Not Rapunzel. Harlow. Jocelyn." I'm having trouble forming sentences.

"Alva, let these innocents go!" Ella cries and I'm impressed again. "It's the royal court you want."

"Now, now, Ella, is that any way to talk to an old friend?" Alva purrs. "Especially one who is so close with one of your fellow princesses? I mean, I'm practically a sister. Or should I say, your new ruler?"

I crouch under the table with the others. I can see Alva putting her arm around Rose, who starts coughing.

"Wicked One, don't you mean *I'm* their new ruler?" Rose's voice is light, but her brow furrows. "We had a deal. You get all the other kingdoms while I rule Enchantasia and keep those delinquents at FTRS locked up to do my bidding. I already have a way to keep them in line."

Alva examines her wickedly long, dark nails. "Rose, dear, if I'm being truthful for a change, I must admit being back here in Royal Manor where I cursed you as an infant makes me long for this kingdom too." She waves a jeweled hand around. "I want them all, darling! And let's be honest. Who are we kidding? You are in no shape to rule! You slept a hundred years! Your reign has been shorter than the others so you have no clue what's going on in your own village!"

"We need to move," I whisper. "Before she knows I'm gone." We begin to crawl over broken glass to get to the other end of the table. I can see the ballroom doors open a few feet away. Closer. Closer. We are going to make it.

"I do too," Rose whines, sounding like one of my little brothers. "We had a deal! I already gave you the girl like you wanted." She points to our table and sees no sign of my body. Her mouth twists in anger. "Where did Gillian Cobbler go?"

I stop short with a shiver. Alva's laugh is so cold that I hear ice cracking in our water goblets. "I should have known you couldn't even manage a task this simple! Boys!" Alva commands her screeching gargoyles. I see one land right at my feet. "Bring her to me!"

CHAPTER 18

Heroes Unite

The gargoyle's rancid breath makes me inhale sharply, and I shrink back as I see its gray claws reach under the table for us. Ollie bats at it with a broken goblet, and the gargoyle screeches and flies away.

"Move! Move!" Ollie cries and we crawl faster and faster, ignoring the cracking sound and the bolts of lightning until they split our table in half. The sides collapse, leaving us out in the open.

"Ah, there she is. Lovely!" Alva says.

I jump up, dragging Maxine and the others with me toward the ballroom doors. They're so close that I can almost touch them. I am not being cursed again. None of us will be.

"Run all you want, child. You'll never escape this room!"

The doors to the ballroom seal shut. "Splendid!" Alva's smile falters. She gestures to a gargoyle. "Seize them!"

"Stop right there, you wicked fairy!"

Holy gingerbread! Is that Jax *and Rapunzel*?

The secret siblings rappel off the second-level balcony and race toward Alva's army of gargoyles, cutting the beasties off from our path.

"We're saved!" Ollie marvels. "Jax is all princely and his sis is a good princess after all!"

Maxine punches him in the arm.

"Did I say 'sister'? I mean, s…s…sassy friend!" Ollie corrects himself.

We watch in awe as Rapunzel and Jax drop to the floor and pull gold swords out of their scabbards. Jax looks dashing as he begins slashing the air and pushing gargoyles back, while Rapunzel pulls radishes out of the pleats of her ball gown and hurls them at the beasties. She looks surprisingly fierce for a princess. I've never seen the royals act so royally! I'm amazed as gargoyles begin dropping like flies, and Jax and Rapunzel soon surround Alva.

"Make a move toward Gilly and my friends, and you'll regret it," Jax tells Alva, holding his sword to her chin.

"And what do we have here? A princess taking orders from a delinquent?" Alva laughs coldly. "Why, this evening just gets more and more interesting!" She zaps two of her sleeping gargoyles and they instantly awaken. "But we can't let the merriment go on forever." The gargoyles hiss and move closer to Rapunzel and Jax, who back into each other with their swords still raised.

"Alva, if you leave now and promise not to touch the other princesses—including foolish Rose—or our guests, we will not harm you," Rapunzel tells her, "but if not, I am afraid you have given us no choice but to fight."

Alva tsks. "Darling, fight all you want. Can't you see I've already won?" She motions to her gargoyles, which are in motion once more. "Take Rose and Gillian away 'til I need them," Alva orders.

"You won't get past us!" Jax tells her.

I don't hesitate. I take off toward the ropes Rapunzel and Jax have left behind and start climbing to the balcony. A gargoyle pulls at my dress, but I kick it off. Maxine, Ollie, and Kayla are right behind me, while Jax and Rapunzel try to fight off gargoyles below.

"No!" Rose cries as a gargoyle swoops down to grab her.

"I won't allow you to get away with this! Alva, you owe me!" Rose screams as the gargoyle lifts her up. "You owe me!" She points to the RLWs. "Royal Ladies-in-Waiting. You have been *charmed*!"

The word sounds strange on Princess Rose's lips, but I soon know why. Maxine's sash flashes and her eyes go slack. RLWs rise, marching toward Alva. The other RLWs fall in line around them, looking straight ahead and standing at attention.

"What the gingerbread is going on?" I hear Ollie yell as Maxine drops from the rope and heads toward the RLWs.

"Those sashes aren't just trackers," I realize. Kayla flies over to Maxine and jumps on her back, but Maxine throws her off. "They've got a spell to make the wearers do Rose's bidding!" Now I understand why Rose wanted the princesses to wear honorary RLW sashes. I spot Ella and Snow joining the ranks of the others. Rapunzel is the only one not wearing a sash, and I'm sure that's because Jax filled her in on our suspicions.

Alva laughs as her gargoyles fly to her side. "So you have an army of pink princesses and wicked little girls, have you? Why would I be afraid of them when I can do this?" Alva begins to conjure a spell right in front of us.

Rose holds up my bag of gingerroot triumphantly. "No dragon morphing for you today, Alva!" She dumps the contents of the bag into her hand and a single petal falls out. "What? No! It can't be gone!"

And that is why Wolfington told us to save it for a good use. Looks like Rose and I both failed tonight.

"Darling, I'm way beyond dragons these days. See for yourself!" Alva's body begins to stretch and spin, her laughter disintegrating into screeches. Fire engulfs her completely. Through the flames I see one leathery green wing, then another, and a spike-covered tail that whips around so fast that it knocks one gargoyle into a wall and squeezes another 'til it shrieks. Scales take over her growing body, and a long, scaly head with gnashing teeth and diamond-shaped yellow eyes pops out. From her mouth comes a plume of fire that toasts the table and several beasties. We drop down from our ropes and rush to a corner to get away.

"She can turn into a wyvern?" Ollie moans. "I thought dragons were bad. Wyverns are even harder to kill. Watch the tail and, um, try not to get torched." We dive out of the way as fire comes too close for comfort.

Jax slides under a wall of fire to reach us. "How do we kill that thing?" Jax yells, grabbing a chair and holding it up like a shield. The embers from a nearby fire ignite his chair, and he drops it like a hot cross bun.

Rapunzel comes running over, dragging Rose behind her like a rag doll. Rapunzel turns and begins to shake her fellow princess. "That wyvern will rip apart the whole castle while the princesses and the others are under her spell! You have to uncharm them so we can get everyone to safety!"

Princess Rose holds her head in her hands. "I can't with all this commotion. There is a dragon in the ballroom. What am I supposed to do? Walk through the flames and ask all the RLWs to hold hands with Ella and Snow and repeat after me the charm that reverses the spell? I'll be a toasted marshmallow before I cross the dance floor!"

"You selfish girl!" Rapunzel scolds. "Were you so desperate for glory that you had to curse your own sisters and your kingdom? How could you work with the fairy that destroyed your life?"

"I thought I could trick her!" Rose cries as flames engulf half the ballroom. I can't even see Maxine or the other RLWs anymore. I can only hope they're okay. "Haven't you ever heard the saying, 'The enemy of your enemy is your friend'? Alva's plan was so delicious. How could I not want to be part of taking you all down and getting the kingdom for myself? I should have known she'd never let Enchantasia be mine—even if I handed over Gillian." Rose glares at me and her eyes look yellow in the flames.

The Evil Queen and Jocelyn weren't lying. They were actually trying to protect me! "You are the poorest excuse for a princess I've ever seen!" I yell.

At that moment, the wyvern's tail curls around Rose's body and lifts her off the ground and away before we can stop it. One of its massive legs knocks down a rear wall of the ballroom, and debris rains down on our heads.

"Rose!" Rapunzel cries as Rose screams in horror. "She's a pill, but I can't let her die. How do we kill that thing?"

For once, I'm completely stumped. "I don't know!" I realize and that terrifies me. What kind of hero am I?

"Houratiempo!" I hear someone yell, and I see Jocelyn and Harlow running toward us. Jocelyn has Jax's pocket watch and is using it to zap the wyvern's legs. The wyvern screeches in anger. The blast holds the creature hostage for a moment, but I know that moment won't last long. Jocelyn hits me in the arm. "I told you we weren't the villains!"

"I see that now!" I shout. "I'm sorry!"

Jocelyn's eyes bulge out of her head. "That's your apology?"

"Jocelyn! Now is not the time to be petty!" Harlow has her back to us, and I wouldn't believe it if I didn't see it with my own eyes. The Evil Queen is commanding the flames *away* from Ella, Snow, Maxine, and the RLWs on the other side of the room. "You don't have much time. This room is going to come down," Harlow yells to us. "You must hit the wyvern in its mouth or the vents behind its legs. The impact should cause Alva to transform back to her natural state and then I may be able to contain her. Use this." She produces a dagger from her skirt pocket. "It's laced with gingerroot. Once she's back in human form, this should hold her for a few minutes."

"*Should* hold?" Rapunzel and Jax ask at the same time. They look at each other.

"Do you have a better idea, Princess?" Harlow snaps. Jocelyn and I duck as a table is thrown past our heads. I notice the wyvern's legs are starting to move again.

"Okay, we'll try it," Rapunzel says as flames shoot in our direction.

Jax throws me out of the way as the fire comes dangerously

close to us. "Lead it away with anything red," Harlow adds. "It hates red."

I scan the room for something red. Of course, we're in a room filled with pink. Then I spot a red velvet tapestry hanging on a wall. "Let's use that!" I tell the others.

Rapunzel freaks. "That tapestry has been in the kingdom for over a hundred years!" A breath of fire crumbles a section of the balcony, and pieces fall on us. "But I guess it's worn out," she says quickly. "I'll go get it."

Jax holds Rapunzel back. "You stay here, Princess. It's too dangerous."

"No!" Rapunzel insists. "This is my kingdom too. We'll fight this beast together."

Jax looks sad, and quickly I realize why. He pulls Maxine's gingerroot bag from his pocket and empties the contents in his hands, blowing them in Rapunzel's face. She freezes on impact. "I'm sorry!" he tells her. "It's for your own good." He looks at Harlow. "Lead the wyvern your way, and we'll grab the tapestry."

We wait 'til Harlow does, then make a break. Jax, Ollie, and Kayla run straight past the beast and begin to tug the tapestry off the wall. Jocelyn and I follow closely behind, but our timing is off. I hear the fire before I smell it. The scent is of rotting flesh and…my skirt! It's on fire! Jocelyn dives on top of me, patting the flames out with her skirt.

"Are you okay?" Jocelyn asks.

"My left leg burns, but I think I'm fine," I tell her. "Thanks."

"Now you owe me two times!" she declares. We look across the room and see that Jax and Ollie have the tapestry down. Part of it gets singed as they run back across the ballroom, but there is enough of the tapestry left to still be useful. Harlow continues to lead the flames in the other direction, while the rest of us gather behind her to discuss our next move.

"Weapon!" I tell Jocelyn as Harlow leads the wyvern away from us again. "I'll throw it. I've got good aim."

Jocelyn holds the dagger close to her chest.

"You're not even on the fencing team!" Jocelyn yells back as Ollie and Jax jump from a flame that Kayla flies above. "Stop trying to be the hero! I'm doing it!"

We hear a screech and turn to see Harlow backed into a corner with the wyvern coming her way. But before anyone can help her, the beast sends a wall of flames in her direction. When the smoke clears, a rocky crater is all that remains in her place.

"Harlow!" Jocelyn cries.

The air is getting thicker and hotter by the second. We won't be able to stand here much longer without Harlow's protection. I think of Maxine on the other side of the room with the princesses that will stand there 'til the walls come down around them or their curse is lifted. Is Rapunzel okay where Jax placed her frozen in a deep corner of the ballroom? How are we going to get out of this crumbling room? Jocelyn is crying too hard to be of much use. Jax sits her down and pulls the dagger from her hands.

"Throw it, thief," he tells me.

I shake my head. "No, Jocelyn's right. I'm no hero. Look at all you guys have done tonight while I screwed everything up. I can't do this!"

Jax puts his hands on my shoulders. "Yes, you can. We're a team, remember? We'll finish this together."

Ollie and Kayla pick up the remains of the tapestry. "We'll distract it," Kayla says. "You throw that dagger with all you've got. Make it a good shot, roomie!"

My hands shake as I hold the cold dagger in my hands. If I screw up, we're finished, but if I do this right, we could save the entire kingdom this time.

"When they get close enough, I'll tell you to throw," Jax says as we run closer to get the best shot. My eyes are on Kayla and Ollie, who are darting between the wyvern's huge, scaly legs.

"Hey, beastie! Over here!" Ollie shouts as Kayla flies above him, holding the tapestry in her hands. The wyvern turns its massive head and screeches so loud that I hear ringing in my ears. I watch as it opens its mouth, exposing its gnashing teeth in seemingly slow motion. It's about to spray my friends with fire.

"Now!" Jax yells as we race into the line of fire behind Kayla.

I stare into the wyvern's orange-and-yellow eyes and Jocelyn's doubts echo in my head. I'm not even on the fencing team. Can I throw this far enough?

I'll have to try. With a feeling of fierce determination, I take aim and throw as hard as I can, sailing the dagger straight into the wyvern's mouth.

The creature screams, then begins to shimmer and freezes with one massive claw in midair before it starts to dissolve in a haze of smoke and flames, leaving behind a bruised and battered wicked fairy. There's no time to grab her. We take cover as the ceiling of Royal Manor rains down in a spectacular display of fire, ashes, and golden embers around us.

Happily Ever After Scrolls

Brought to you by FairyWeb—magically appearing on scrolls throughout Enchantasia for the past ten years!

BREAKING NEWS:

Alva Captured! Princess Rose in Custody! Fairy Tale Reform School Students Save the Day (Again)!

by Beatrice Beez

Happily Ever After Scrolls is pleased to confirm that Alva has been captured! In an alarming twist, Princess Rose has been taken into custody for her involvement in the reign of terror that has befallen our kingdom. While details are sketchy, palace sources say Rose planned to take over Enchantasia from her fellow princesses with Alva's help. Using charmed sashes, she cursed her RLWs and fellow princesses to do her bidding, but was thwarted by Rapunzel and FTRS student Jax Porter.

"We are taking the matter of Princess Rose into our own hands," says Rapunzel. "She will be dealt with by her fellow princesses and take a leave of absence while we discuss her behavior. We couldn't have stopped her without help from the Fairy Tale Reform School students." May we suggest Rose be sentenced to a transformation at Fairy Tale Reform School?

Meanwhile, in a fit of rage, Alva turned into a wyvern, a type of dragon that is impossible to kill. Thanks to the quick thinking of the FTRS students, she was struck by a dagger laced with gingerroot and returned to her fairy form where the Evil Queen contained her. It turns out Professor Harlow was working undercover with Headmistress Flora at FTRS to capture Alva the whole time! "After she transformed back to her wicked fairy form, Alva was turned into a statue by Professor Harlow and stored at an undisclosed location where she will be heavily guarded," Headmistress Flora tells us. "We at FTRS will make sure she is never a threat to the kingdom of Enchantasia again."

With Harlow's name cleared, she will likely take her position back at FTRS, which leaves Blackbeard in the lurch. "We'll find room for everyone," Miri, the school spokesmirror, says.

Once again, Enchantasia residents have Gillian Cobbler to thank for their safety! Or do they?

"I cannot take credit for the events at Royal Manor

yesterday evening," says Gillian, recovering in the school infirmary from burns from the wyvern. "Princess Rapunzel and my friends—Jax, Ollie, Kayla, Maxine, and Jocelyn— did far more than I ever could," she says. "The only way to beat someone as fierce as Alva or as distressed as Princess Rose is to work together as a team. FTRS has taught me that, and I'm grateful to my friends for saving the day."

CHAPTER 19

A New Path

Gillian Cobbler—For your epic bravery in the war against Alva, we grant you early release from Fairy Tale Reform School.

—Signed this day by Headmistress Flora

I can't believe it! I'm free! I'm going home! When the scroll arrived under our dorm room door this morning, I could barely contain my excitement. Even Kayla was jumping up and down. And that was before Maxine barged in.

"Look what I got!" Maxine held up a piece of parchment with the new FTRS school emblem stamped on it. Now our school crest has five boxes—a full moon, a trident, a bitten apple, a glass slipper, and a skull and crossbones. With the truth about Harlow out, Blackbeard was given a much more suitable position. He's now FTRS's official head of athletics and safety.

Kayla read Maxine's pardon. I suspected we'd soon see more pardons coming for Ollie and Jax. "This is great," she said, her wings popping out and beginning to flutter. "I'm so happy for both of you."

I give my roommate a hug. Now I'm getting misty. "We're not done yet." I look into her amber eyes. "We won't stop 'til we find your family too."

Our room's mirror begins to glow violet, then fuchsia. "Illegal use of magic! Occupant in upper-level dorm room not permitted." Miri says. Ogres aren't usually allowed on upper floors of the girls' dormitory due to the weight limit.

"Miri?" I say. "Kayla and I are with Maxine. She was visiting."

"Oh!" The hue of Miri's mirror turns a soothing shade of lavender. "Madame Cleo was looking for you three. I'll patch her through."

The mirror swirls fade and Madame Cleo comes into focus. She's sitting on a rock with waves lapping around her.

"Morning, darlings!" Her aquamarine tail flaps against the black boulder. Her long, beautiful hair is a lovely shade of amber, which matches her shell top. "Blackbeard and I wanted to congratulate you all on a job well done with Alva." Blackbeard's large frame comes into view. His ship is docked right behind Madame Cleo.

"Jolly good job ye all did! Ye be quite the crew," he says in a booming voice. "Before ye set sail, we be inviting ye to a party on my ship. We set sail in one hour! The lads and the other professors will be joining us. Come packed and then we'll see you off."

A pirate party? I'm so there. "We just got our notices. I didn't know we'd be leaving so soon."

"Your families have been informed," Madame Cleo tells us, and Maxine instinctively clutches my hand. "Is that okay, darlings? Who doesn't want to be sprung from reform school as soon as possible?"

I've been dying to get out of here and yet...I look around my room. The drawings Kayla and I have hung, the paper stars that dangle from the ceiling, my comfy bed, the stained glass window, the mini magical chalkboard that hangs on the back of our door. Who will be Kayla's roommate? Will she like her as much as me? What will everyone do now that there's no villain to go after?

"We've told yer parents we'd send ye home by Pegasi, well, except for the bonny Miss Maxine. You'll be traveling by coach." Maxine nods. "You'll leave straight from the party." Blackbeard jumps over the rail of his ship and lands in the water next to Madame Cleo's rock. She squeals as he climbs up next to her. "See you soon!" The mirror goes dark as he puts an arm around our teacher. Gross.

"I guess I should go pack," Maxine says uncertainly. "I can't believe I'm going home." She tugs at one of the necklaces around her neck. "I don't even remember what life was like in my village. At least the ogres have signed that peace treaty with the princesses. Life should be better there now. Still, it's going to be nowhere near as fun as being with you guys." She smiles uncertainly. "We'll stay in touch, won't we?"

Fiddlesticks, I'm going to cry. "That's what the Pegasus Post is for! We'll write and maybe we'll even have a reunion."

"A Fairy Tale Reform School Reunion!" Kayla agrees. "I'll plan one since I'll still be here."

"But not for long," I say firmly.

"Not for long," Kayla echoes.

∗✳∗

An hour later, I'm standing at the dock next to Blackbeard's ship and I can hear the merriment and music. Mermaids are swimming around the boat with Madame Cleo, who is sunning herself on a rock, and the pirates on board are clinking glasses and cheering. Pegasi and magic carpets fly overhead, sprinkling confetti. This is one big party.

"They're here!" I hear a pirate shout. "Land ahoy! Leave yer trunk next to the others." I notice two others already there. "Then come aboard, lasses!"

A plank slides out of the side of Blackbeard's ship and lowers to the dock. We hold hands to stay steady and head up the plank. As soon as we reach the deck, we see our professors. Headmistress Flora is with her daughters. Wolfington is talking to Jax, and Ollie is doing a jig with some of the crew. For a moment, I'm confused when I see two individuals dressed in black on the deck. Harlow and Jocelyn look slightly out of place among all the dancing pirates. But I gasp when I catch sight of Jax. He's wearing a royal uniform with a royal gold crest. He looks like a prince! He *is* a prince! I'm stunned.

He bows to me. "I clean up nicely, don't I?"

"You look very royal," I agree. "So you're going home?"

He nods. "Father and I told Rapunzel everything after the attack. She was stunned but very happy. They've got their hands full at the Manor at the moment with Princess Rose." He rolls his eyes. "She says she was under some charm, but I think Ella is wise to her. Either way, she's in a comfy dungeon at the palace until they figure out how to handle her."

"Well, don't rule out reformation," Professor Wolfington says and winks at me. "As we've learned, even the darkest villains can be redeemed."

"Maybe," says Jax, adjusting the gold collar on his dress clothes. "I guess we'll see when I get there." He makes a face. "Father says once he introduces me to everyone, I'm being enrolled at Royal Academy."

"You'll love it!" Dahlia gushes. "All the best people go there."

"All the best students go *here*," Headmistress Flora corrects her.

"Yes they do!" Ollie dances over to me and swings me under his arm. "We did it!" Maxine, Kayla, and Jax join us.

"*You guys* did it," I correct him. "You're the true heroes."

Father sent a Pegasus Post yesterday saying how proud he was of me working with the team. I'm not going to get the praise from others that I got from him this time around, but that's okay. Being a hero is a lot of work. I'm just glad my family is okay, and that with Rose being dealt with, Father's business is still intact.

"You're all heroes," Headmistress Flora corrects me, "and Enchantasia owes you its gratitude." Professor Wolfington passes around glasses of a purple fizzy drink that looks so delicious I want to swallow it in one gulp. The headmistress looks at me. "I'm sorry we had to keep you all in the dark. I know it didn't put me in the best light."

"I understand." I read the *HEAS* this morning too. The wickedest witch ever is actually good and was sending Maxine clues to find the mole and help stop Alva. And I repaid her bravery by freezing her. *Gulp.* "I'm sorry I doubted you." My eyes shift to Professor Harlow and Jocelyn. "Both of you."

"It's understandable," Professor Harlow says in her

smooth-as-silk voice that still makes me shiver. "Not everyone can be as enlightened as Jocelyn and see through the charade."

And that is why she's my least favorite professor here. Still, I owe her my gratitude. "Thank you for trying to save us," I add humbly.

She smiles ever so thinly. "I knew my skills would come in handy with the wyvern. Now that Alva is a statue and locked away, we shall worry about her no more."

Statue or no statue, the thought of Alva still out there makes me nervous.

"You never explained how you got away from the wyvern's flames," Ollie says.

Professor Harlow laughs. "I disappeared before Alva could get anywhere near me. It's just that in the heat my spell took me a little farther away than the ballroom. Still, you did the job well, I must say."

Ollie bows to her. "I guess that's why I get a week's vacation before I head home." He looks at us. "Blackbeard is taking me on a voyage."

"Yes," Blackbeard says. "Madame Cleo and me thought ye could use a vacation after all this ruckus. We're heading to the Enchanted Sea to visit the Little Mermaid."

"We're such good friends now," says Madame Cleo, and I realize she's being beamed from the nearby water in a hand-held mirror in Headmistress Flora's hands. "I'm long overdue for a visit." She wags a finger at us. "Don't you lot go too long without coming to see us, darlings."

"We'll miss you all greatly, but it's time to let you go," Flora agrees. "You've more than proven you're ready to be reintroduced to the kingdom. I'm so proud."

Kayla starts to sniffle. Maxine pulls her in for a hug.

"We haven't forgotten you either, Kayla," Flora says, her face clouding over. "Rumpel is proving tricky to deal with, but I hope we can strike a deal with him to find your family and end his protection over the school in an amicable matter." She looks uncomfortable. "Until then, we hope you'll consider staying on with us at FTRS."

"You mean, I'm not being kicked out?" Kayla asks, her voice trembling.

"On the contrary," Flora says. "To be honest, I feel you still have work to do after all your, shall we say, unsavory business a few months back with Gottie. You will have a home with us until you no longer need it. You needn't even stay in the dorms anymore if you don't want a new roommate."

"Well, you'll still have a roommate," Jocelyn pipes up. "I mean, if you want one. Harlow and I thought you could stay in our quarters with us."

"It will give us a chance to work on leads to your family," Harlow says. "Jocelyn and I are experts at complicated enchantments and location spells."

Kayla looks from me to them in amazement. "I think I'd like that. Thank you!"

Harlow semi-smiles. "You're much obliged."

"Set sail, captain?" a pirate says.

Blackbeard looks at his watch. "I think we can party a little bit longer, don't ye lads think?" Everyone nods. "But ye should ready the ship." He tips his hat to me. "I best be saying me good-byes. We shall meet again though. I sure hope we do."

"We all do." Ollie gives me a hug before he goes off to help the other pirates prepare for the voyage.

Maxine squeezes a little too hard. Kayla flutters over and Jax piles in. I reach for Jocelyn and she jumps in shock.

"Criminals for life," Jax teases.

"*Reformed* criminals," Maxine corrects him.

"I wouldn't have it any other way," I agree. "Being straight and narrow my whole life would have been boring."

"It will still be boring," Kayla says. "We need to have *a little* fun."

"Not too much fun," I hear Flora say, and I smile. I know I'll have just enough.

An hour later, Macho is giving me one last flight, and this time he's landing right in front of my boot. A crowd has gathered outside and they cheer when I dismount. I give Macho a carrot and pet his snout. "I'll miss you," I say and he neighs in agreement. "Don't be a stranger." I watch him take off again and wait 'til he soars over the treetops and the row of boots and teakettles before I head inside my door.

When I do, I'm surprised to see it's changed somewhat. There are new couches, new wallpaper, and even a tarp hanging near the kitchen. *Extension*, it reads. Our boot is getting an expansion? Business must still be good! What haven't changed are the seven people waiting for me.

"Gilly!" Han is the first to grab my legs. Hamish, Felix, Trixie, Father, and Mother complete the sandwich. Well, almost.

"I'm so glad you're home." Anna kisses my cheek.

"Me too." But in the back of my mind, I realize I'm still longing for FTRS. How strange when I wanted to get out for so long. "I'm so glad to see you all." I lock eyes with Father.

"Let's celebrate," he says with a smile. "Mother has made a cake in your honor."

"And we're having roast beef for dinner," Felix says in amazement.

It's a whole new world in the Cobbler household.

"It's all to honor you, our transformed little thief," Mother says. "Our hero."

I smile because I know the truth. I'm still a little bit bad, a lot good, and a whole lot of other things too. Just as it should be.

Pegasus Postal Service

Flying Letters Since The Troll War!

FROM: Prince Jackson Jax (Royal Manor)

TO: Gillian Cobbler (2 Boot Way)

Thief,

I know it's been a few months, but guess who I heard from? Kayla. Looks like Flora is regretting that deal with Rumpelstiltskin. Apparently he's been seen around FTRS a few times, and rumor has it he wants a job there. (Not that you heard that from me. Blame Jocelyn. She's apparently the one who blabbed to Kayla who told Maxine who told Ollie who told me and now I you.)

There's no way we can trust that troll to work at Fairy Tale Reform School. Kayla is itching to get her hands on Rumpel, as you know, and we can't let her tackle that problem on her own, can we? Ollie, Maxine, and I are thinking of getting thrown back into FTRS to help her out. Royal Academy is Dullsville, and I could use a little adventure.

Any chance you'd like to join us?

Who's Who in Enchantasia

Headmistress Flora: Remember that whole glass slipper business with Cinderella? Flora is Princess Ella's formerly wicked stepmother. Now she runs Fairy Tale Reform School.

Professor Wolfington: Little Red Riding Hood has nothing to fear from this former big bad wolf. The only howling he does these days is when a student gets good grades in his history class at FTRS.

Madame Cleo: She made the Little Mermaid's life under the sea miserable, but these days the classy mermaid with the killer hair teaches charm classes and dance at FTRS.

She's also got a bit of a short-term memory problem, which means detention is sometimes forgotten about!

Professor Harlow: Snow White's Evil Queen is still, well, kind of mean, but she means well now that she teaches FTRS students psychology and how to deal with their feelings.

Gottie: Remember the baddie who stuck Rapunzel in that tower? She's still bad, still on the loose, and she's looking for revenge on the princesses and kingdom of Enchantasia. Shiver!

Alva: Sleeping Beauty's dreamcaster could be alive or she could be dead. No one's seen her in years and they're glad. She's the scariest fairy villain in the kingdom.

Blackbeard: The most fearsome pirate to sail the seas is now taking up post at FTRS in Professor Harlow's old job, but he's got a rather unusual way of dealing with student issues—he makes them duel!

Rumpelstiltskin: The baddest of the bad, no one knows much about this mystery wish granter...for now.

Acknowledgments

Pirates, ogres, wicked fairies, and evil manifestos…the world of Fairy Tale Reform School is *almost* too much fun to work on, and that's because of #AwesomeAubrey, a.k.a. Aubrey Poole, my incredible editor who finds the magic and the mischief as fun to create as I do. Thanks for being the most amazing partner a writer could ask for. I'm tickled pink to be on this charming journey with you. (Hmm…maybe I've spent too much time writing about Princess Rose!)

When editing is done, I'm sent off to the capable hands of Alex Yeadon and Kathryn Lynch, the marketing and publicity geniuses who made sure the Fairy Tale Reform School series is seen and heard about in every boot, bookstore, and teakettle nationwide. Thank you to the entire team at Sourcebooks who have given this series such a tremendous amount of love and dedication. To production editor Elizabeth Boyer, thanks for making sure I've got things just right, and to designer Mike Heath, who continues to floor me with the most spectacular covers!

Laura Dail and Tamar Rydzinski, thank you for helping the Fairy Tale Reform School series find a good home both here and on foreign shores, and to my agent Dan Mandel for continuing to steer my pirate ship in the right direction.

Elizabeth Eulberg is the best first reader a writer could ask for. Thanks for all the advice on my villains and reform school students. To Kieran Scott, Jennifer E. Smith, Courtney Sheinmel, Katie Sise, Sarah Mlynowski, Tiffany Schmidt, and Julia DeVillers, thanks for all the writing support and love.

My family—Mike, Tyler, Dylan, and our resident Chihuahua pirate, Captain Jack Sparrow—supports my dreams and encourages me in ways I could never imagine. I love you all so much.

And to the readers—when I started thinking about a school run by former villains, I never could have imagined your wonderful reactions to Gilly and her mixed-up friends and foes. I feel so charmed that you've let Fairy Tale Reform School be part of your world!

About the Author

Jen Calonita is the author of the Secrets of My Hollywood Life series and other books like *Sleepaway Girls* and *Summer State of Mind*, but Fairy Tale Reform School is her first middle-grade series. She rules Long Island, New York, with her husband, Mike; princes, Tyler and Dylan; and Chihuahua, Captain Jack Sparrow, but the only castle she'd ever want to live in is Cinderella's at Walt Disney World.